CAREFREE GARDENING

Carefree Gardening

by

MARGERY FISH

With a foreword by

Anthony Huxley

faber and faber

LONDON · BOSTON

First published in Great Britain in 1966
by W. H. & L. Collingridge Ltd
Reissued in 1972 by David and Charles (Publishers) Ltd
This paperback edition first published in 1989
by Faber and Faber Limited
3 Queen Square London WCIN 3AU
Reprinted 1990

Printed in Great Britain by
Richard Clay Ltd, Bungay, Suffolk

British Library Cataloguing in Publication Data is available

ISBN 0–571–15325–9

Contents

Illustrations

Line Drawings

All the photographs in the book were taken by Pat Brindley. The cover photograph was taken by Jacqui Hurst.

Foreword

Anthony Huxley

Though most gardening books are written by men, household names among authors are somehow more likely to be women— among the first, Jane Loudon with her *Gardening for Ladies* in 1840, followed in the same year by Louisa Johnson with *Every Lady Her Own Flower Gardener*, very much a trend-setting title. Then in due course came others: Gertrude Jekyll, Vita Sackville-West, Eleanour Sinclair Rohde, Frances Perry and Beth Chatto are just some of them. In this assemblage Margery Fish has a very special place.

What is perhaps most astonishing about her is that she came to gardening quite late in life, after a business career. She had little more than twenty years to learn about gardening and to practise it, let alone to write her eight books. She wrote as she gardened, with immense enthusiasm; but she was a meticulous gardener, always inquiring from her friends about plants new to her, experimenting with them in different conditions and observing their qualities.

I met Margery Fish when I was helping to edit *Amateur Gardening* magazine. How different she was from most of our authors! Her sentences rushed almost uncontrollably along her pages, with little respect for punctuation. I'm afraid I used to groan when it came to editing her pieces, but it was soon plain that, once those pieces were tidied up, readers certainly responded to their exuberant approach so clearly based on the writer's practical experience, and mentioning so many relatively unfamiliar plants.

Her books are in no way set out for reference, though—as here in *Carefree Gardening*—they are divided into chapters almost like individual magazine articles. This means that every sentence must be savoured if one wants to obtain real value from the experience she records. But what a worthwhile exercise that still remains! Margery Fish's aim, as set out in her original introduction, was 'to strive for a natural effect and aim at producing in the garden what nature does outside, but with cultivated plants'. Her text is as relevant today as it was in 1966.

Introduction

Our gardening ways are changing. Instead of trying to make our gardens as different as possible from nature we now strive for a natural effect and aim at producing in the garden what nature does outside, but with cultivated plants.

When plants are allowed to grow naturally they make a harmonious picture and the result is a happy garden, and a happy garden is a peaceful one, with a backbone of plants that go on from year to year. The continual upheaval caused by seasonal bedding and unbedding gives no feeling of permanence and the effect can be very artificial. Annual and bedding plants can be used in a permanent framework and then become part of the garden.

A good garden can be made with plants that do not require constant attention. We are all striving to have a garden as labour saving as possible and with a natural garden this can be done. With informal planting there is not so much urgency in doing the seasonal work and by careful planning one can have a garden that not only looks attractive but can also be kept up with the minimum of trouble.

CHAPTER ONE

Natural Borders

My idea of a natural border is one where all the plants grow happily together, often intermingling with each other. There is nothing forced or artificial about it, in fact it is just as nature would have planted it. It should look good at whatever time of year you happen to look at it, whether in the height of summer or in the middle of winter.

I remember seeing a narrow border in a friend's garden for the first time on a winter's day, when the plants were rimed with frost and there were only the shapes of the plants to see. I was glad that nothing had been trimmed or cut down, and that instead of a bare strip of soil there were mounds of feathery foliage. The border was at the top of a low wall so nepeta had been planted at the edge, and its sparkling stems were foaming over the wall. Irises stood up proudly, *Geum borisii* had grown to a large plant and its crinkled dark leaves looked lovely outlined in white.

The shrubby potentillas are ideal for a natural border; they grow informally in nature and planted near the edge of a wall they fall casually over the edge. There are many good varieties and several of the *fruticosa* forms are ideal for this kind of border. *P. f. farreri* is seldom higher than 2 feet and has bright golden flowers. It seems to be nearly always in flower and is a good friend, for even when the flowers are over the bush looks quite pleasant without the flowers. *P. f. mandshurica* is low and spreading in the same way and also produces its flowers—white in this case—for many months on mats of grey foliage which looks darker than it is because of the purplish stems. The flowers of *P. arbuscula* are a cross between the two, the colour being paler than in *P. farreri*. This is rather a shaggy bush, bigger than the others but just as generous with its flowers.

For a big border *Kolkwitzia amabilis* is a graceful shrub that looks at home with low-growing geraniums and I like to see it with a tangle of *Geranium nodosum* or *G. endressii* Wargrave playing round its feet. Its arching stems look lovely whether furnished with leaves or not. The border I saw that wintry day was bright with bergenias and against the phantom plants their glossy leaves in crimson and orange were very much alive. In spring and summer bulbous plants furnish extra interest. Daffodils and tulips are good in spring and though the wild *Gladiolus byzantinus* can be a nuisance with its seeding, groups mixed with kolkwitzia or a white-flowered potentilla can be very satisfying. I grow the tall *G. purpureo-auratus*, which flowers in the autumn and goes on till November. It is taller than *byzantinus* and its delicate grey-mauve flowers are good with everything. Though quite hardy in places near London and further afield it can be very coy about flowering. I remember one year, when it dug in its heels and refused to produce a single flower for me, I went to see the little garden of a friend and there was my gladiolus blooming away like an old resident although I had given it to her only a very short time before. That gave me the idea that it might prefer shade, for it was growing in shade in my friend's garden. Some I planted under the light shade of an apple-tree flower magnificently, others under a willow are not backward either, so the shady end of the border would seem to be the best place for it.

Shrubs and heathers are ideally suited and have a completely natural look. I admired such a border in a garden in Sevenoaks. The lower branches of a large *Elaeagnus pungens aurea* were sweeping a wide planting of *Erica carnea* in various colours, and nearby a smoke bush, *Cotinus coggygria* (*Rhus cotinus*), was light and filmy against the neat shiny leaves of the elaeagnus; and in spring there are deep blue scillas. *Anthemis cupaniana* combines well with the cotinus, and it could well have been used in this harmonious planting, its silvery mat of foliage being covered with white daisies for many a long day.

Hellebores are particularly valuable for the winter and one in particular, *Helleborus corsicus*, (now said to be *H. lividus corsicus*), is a good all-the-year plant for a place in the garden that is in constant use. I noticed a very happy and very natural treatment of a bed next to the porch of a front door. Against the white wall of the house a tall plant of golden privet (*Ligustrum ovalifolium aureo-marginatum*) showed up magnificently, and in front a large clump of *H. corsicus* filled in all the spaces, with wide fans of *Cotoneaster horizontalis* spreading out on either side. I saw this planting in September and white Japanese anemones on tall stems made a lovely finish. Anemones are easy, good-tempered plants that need little attention but they are inclined to run slightly so must not be planted where this would make trouble. The white variety of martagon lily, *Lilium regale* or Solomon's Seal (*Polygonatum multiflorum*) would be ideal for a summer finish and in spring the tall arching stems of *Leucojum aestivum* Gravetye Variety would make a background for the hellebore.

A north border in a Wiltshire garden was particularly good in autumn with hardy fuchsias growing with different types of hydrangeas. Variegated forms of both fuchsias and hydrangeas were a happy change among the others, and Japanese anemones in white, pale pink and really dark pink were lovely. In spring a fine show of tulips made the bed colourful, and really it required very little work to keep it going.

I have mentioned heathers before and shall do so again because they look after themselves so completely and fit into any kind of picture. A bed of azaleas in a garden I know has Crown Imperials (*Fritillaria imperialis*) planted among them and is carpeted with ericas and the little, purple-leaved violet, *Viola labradorica*. Heathers are good with conifers too, and I always admire a bed in the garden of a friend in Lancashire who has planted different types of silver birch as a background for heathers grown with conifers. *Erica carnea* Springwood is beautiful with *Thuya occidentalis* Rheingold, with wild primroses or the little primrose-coloured polyanthus Lady Greer nestling nearby. In his acid soil this gardener can grow the beautiful calluna, Mrs Pat, a form of *C. vulgaris* which has foliage so beautiful that there is no need for it to flower; in fact I have never noticed its flowers. I grow this enchantress in a bed of greensand and I love the silvery variegation of its foliage and the bright pink tips of the shoots. A good companion would be one of the blue pulmonarias, either *P. angustifolia azurea* or *P.* Munstead Blue. The pink form of *Erica carnea* Springwood is also good with blue pulmonarias and is more informal in its growth than Mrs Pat and turns the bed into a pleasant tangle of soft pink and delicate foliage with the dark green and piercing blue of the pulmonaria. In the same garden I enjoyed the tall hybrid *Erica* Arthur Johnson growing with *Rhododendron praecox*. This erica, which will tolerate lime if required, has deep pink flowers, and the flowers of the rhododendron are lavender-pink. The picture was completed by drifts of soft blue scillas.

Some natural plantings come about by accident and are better than if we had taken endless trouble to achieve a carefree effect. Nature's planting is often better than ours. In my ditch garden a fine self-sown plant of *Geranium psilostemon* (*G. armenum*) appeared under a willow. I have always grown it in full sun but its magenta flowers are more intense in the shade. Next to it another geranium, Clarice Druce, had put itself at the top of a bank and its luxuriant mass of dark foliage made a happy covering for the lower—often bare—part of *G. psilostemon*. *G.* Clarice Druce is, I understand, a cross between *G. endressii* and *G. striatum* and the large pink flowers are faintly etched like *striatum*. On the other side of *G. psilostemon, Potentilla* Miss Willmott has kindly sown herself, and her long stems with their bright pink flowers found their way to add another shade of pink to the shades of the geranium flowers. Miss Wilmott is my favourite among the *nepalensis* types, not only because it sows itself so freely and flowers until November, but because of the colour of the flowers. Some nurseries describe the colour as carmine, others as cherry-red, but neither seems quite to fit it. I have heard it described in America as 'Russian' pink but no one in England knows what is meant by that description. I have an oriental bathroom mat with just that colour mixed with scarlet and black and primrose, and when I wanted towels to match the nearest the shop assistants could get to the colour was old rose. So perhaps that is the right description. Whatever the colour is called it is a warm deep pink and the flowers have a crimson spot on each petal and brown anthers.

One does not often see the blue-flowered herbaceous *Clematis heracleaefolia* grown with other plants, although it mingles most naturally with many other good things. It is not a plant that should be staked too firmly and I like to see it all mixed up with its neighbours. I grow one large clump in a bed under a glaucous Atlantic cedar, and in the same bed is the white-flowered *Lysimachia clethroides* and a soft pink *Anemone hupehensis*, which was given to me as the species and not one of the hybrids. These three plants flower at the same time, in early autumn. The anemone runs mildly, the lysimachia does not run but the roots take the form of long underground stems which radiate from the crown. The clematis does not run either but its tall stems are gregarious and hobnob with their neighbours in a most engaging way. The foliage of the lysimachia makes wonderful autumn colour, that of the clematis is inclined to become golden before it shrivels and that of the anemone remains a strong dark green.

In the same part of the garden other plants have intermingled to make a close cover of foliage and flower. I planted the pink cow parsley, *Pimpinella magna rosea*, and it has since seeded itself here and there. It makes a much more solid clump of dark ferny foliage than the wayside variety and the 2-foot stems are not so upright as those we see in the hedgerows. The flowers are really rather a dirty shade of pink though I see the colour is described as 'warm' pink in catalogues. It has rather more blue in it than a real pink but although I do not rave about the plant—as a friend from Plymouth once did—I like its old-world dowdiness and find it makes a happy picture with *Campanula burghaltii* with its large hanging bells in shaded slaty blue. Nature helped by sowing *C. lactiflora* in various shades of blue, and *Polemon-*

ium caeruleum, which is rather too rich a blue for the cow parsley. If I had thought of polemonium in this connection I would have chosen the pale blue *P. lanatum humile* or the flesh-pink *P. carneum*, which is less tight in its habit and has pleasant variations in the colour of its flowers. One of the best plants to use in autumn is *Polygonum campanulatum*. It does not run like some polygonums but makes a thick carpet of good foliage at ground level. The tiny pink flowers on 2-foot stems last for weeks and mix well with grasses, lilies or any other flowers.

Nothing beats the combination of yellow and white and for a happy tangle that will take care of itself for most of the summer I put the white *Achillea* W. B. Child and the yellow *Achillea* Moonshine near each other with *Alchemilla mollis* in the foreground. The white achillea is much neater than the roaming *A. ptarmica* and has different type flowers. Instead of white buttons they are little white-centred daisies and the foliage is rather ferny. The silver-leaved *A.* Moonshine flowers on and on and so does the green-flowered alchemilla.

In a big shady bed large plants of *Helleborus corsicus* will join up with others of like stature. In a triangular bed between a west and a north wall my plants of *H. corsicus* have grown enormously and are as big as the great plants of *Euphorbia mellifera* and *wulfenii* that grow there. This is a very green corner in the winter, with the green flowers of the helleborus and the apple-green and blue-green of the euphorbias. Golden flowers on a gold-variegated *Jasminum nudiflorum* on the wall behind enliven the scene. In April the dwarf almond *Prunus tenella* Fire Hill makes a thicket of slender stems alive with fiery pink flowers. A little later the purplish-pink flowers of *Indigofera gerardiana* add colour, and in autumn a large clump of *Curtonus paniculatus* (*Antholyza paniculata*) fills the background with deep bronze-orange flowers. The foliage of this plant turns gold after the flowers are over and keeps its colour for many weeks.

CHAPTER TWO

The Ageless Ones

The ideal border for a carefree garden is one planted with subjects that can be left to look after themselves. They will not want dividing, because they do not increase fast, in fact all they ask is to be left alone. Staking can be reduced to a minimum if they are given taller, stronger companions who will be ready with protecting arms and solid comforting stems.

It is quite safe to plant *Hacquetia epipactis* in a border that is not going to be disturbed. I should hesitate to grow it among michaelmas daisies, golden rod or the early doronicums, which spread so quickly, and I always play for safety by tucking it away at the bottom of a dwarf wall, where it gets protection and shade, and can sleep safely in the winter. There is no worry after the green and gold flowers have opened at ground level, like little bright flower-heads that have been dropped by mistake. After that the leaves will come and the flower stems will grow to 6 or 8 inches, and that thick bunch of shamrock leaves and eyeless green calyces make an attractive background feature for summer flowers. It can be broken up quite safely after it has finished flowering, particularly if one chooses a spell of damp weather.

Another of the early stalwarts in my garden is *Mertensia virginica*, sometimes called 'Virginian Cowslip' and allied to pulmonaria. It disappears completely after flowering so it needs to be well protected by really strong roots as well as solid stems and firm foliage. I grow mine with pink cow parsley, a plebian plant if ever there was one, but an attractive self-reliant creature which is informality itself. The leaves of the mertensia are glaucous with touches of deep blue as they first come through and the china blue flowers unfurl like the fronds of a fern. The bright green foliage of the cow parsley is as finely cut as a delicate fern, and the pink flowers are quite deep in colour but not at all bright. The two plants intermingle pleasantly, the cow parsley flowering after the mertensia.

An early and original little plant one seldom sees but which is easy and not invasive is good for the front of the border. We used to know *Lathyrus vernus* as *Orobus vernus*, and its rounded clump of tiny leaves is absolutely covered with flowers in early spring. The one I like best is *L. v. albo-roseus*, with pea-like flowers which are partly white and partly salmon-pink. The ordinary type is more like a vetch, in fact the colloquial name for this lathyrus is Spring Bitter Vetch and the colour of the flowers is deep violet-blue, shaded like the pink and white form. Two colours that are not shaded are the white form and a brilliant blue species called *cyaneus*. These plants are neat growing and seem to deal with their dead flowers without help from me. Certainly I have never done more than admire them.

Another lovely spring flower that must not be disturbed is the Bleeding Heart (*Dicentra spectabilis*), also known as the Lyre plant or Lady-in-the-Bath. It looks delicate with its beautifully cut glaucous leaves, and its pink lockets dangling from translucent stems. As a matter of fact it is quite tough, although its roots are as brittle as glass and need very careful handling. It likes a little shade and I give it Solomon's Seal as a companion. The dicentra does well with a wall behind it and the Solomon's Seal (*Polygonatum multiflorum*) arches gracefully from the wall.

The dwarf dicentras are easier to please. They run about and increase well, also preferring a little shade, and they flower even longer than *D. spectabilis*. There is no question of finding support for them for *D. eximia*, in pink or white, is usually under a foot. The deeper pink *D.* Bountiful—a form of *D. formosa*—has larger flowers and is slightly taller. It also flowers again in the autumn.

I should have hesitated to mention *Aceriphyllum rossii* in this book had I not discovered it in the catalogue of a well-known rock garden nursery. Let me say at once that it is not a spectacular plant but one of those unshowy but interesting ones we are inclined to forget until we see them given high praise in a catalogue or magazine article. Then we realise how ungrateful we have been, run up to make amends and show them off to our friends for a few days until something more exciting comes out.

My poor aceriphyllum moulders its life away leaning against the base of a sundial and is nearly smothered by a *Daphne mezereum* on one side, and a fascinating white-tipped juniper (*Juniperus chinensis expansa variegata*) on the other. Above it a very healthy small-leaved ivy—*Hedera helix sagittifolia*—is strangling everything in sight, and for good measure a golden sage, which has put on weight over the years, is also crowding the poor aceriphyllum. And yet it survives, and it has done so for over 20 years. It is a Korean alpine plant, said to be fairly common on the Diamond Mountains. It is of the saxifrage persuasion with dark, sharp-pointed leaves like a maple and flat heads of cream flowers on strong stems. Its heavy woody rhizomes grow slowly and when it is growing strongly pieces can be broken off to make new plants. As I write I feel inspired to start chiselling bits off my aceriphyllum and perhaps build up another planting where it will have a chance to be seen and admired. I hope I shall act before other plants come into flower which require attention. In some pursuits one can catch up with jobs that are not done at the right time, but not in gardening. There is usually only one time when the work can be done and if it is crowded out by other things it means waiting till the same time next year!

About the beginning of May one notices that the burning bush plant, *Dictamnus albus* (*D. fraxinella*) is growing strongly and getting ready for its flowering in June and July. It is rather slow-growing and takes several years to grow into a sizeable clump. It is definitely not one of the plants from which one can take off bits to give one's friends. There are two ways of propagating it, by seed or by chopping up its fleshy roots in the spring. The root cuttings produce plants more quickly than seed of course, but to get them it means disturbing the plant and perhaps losing a season's flowers. I cannot imagine anyone having enough dictamnus to do this so I would buy my plants from a nursery. Dictamnus is a very well-behaved plant for a border, it grows up straight and strong, needs no staking, and is good value from mid-April to November, for the early leaves and forming buds are attractive, and after the flowers are over the seed pods almost look like buds. I can never bring myself to cut down those handsome spikes, but I have often thought they would look well in a dried flower arrangement.

Dictamnus purpurescens is rosy-purple, with pencillings in a deeper shade and *D. albus* is an elegant white form. In both cases the stamens are long and conspicuous. Divided leaves, which are slightly fragrant, make this a neat and satisfactory plant. I have never had enough courage to see if it really justifies its name of Burning Bush by trying to light the inflammable oil which is exuded from the glands on the flower stalks. I am told one needs a hot still evening for the experiment.

Not so sturdy or solid as a clump, catananche is a slow-growing plant that needs no attention when once established. Its leaves are narrow and the flowers grow on slender stalks about 2½ feet high. To me the charm of the plant is mainly in the overlapping silver bracts which encase the calyx. Before the flowers open silver buds sway gently in the wind, and when the flowers appear they too have great character, with blunt blue petals, with deeper markings. The white-flowered form is lovely too.

Another plant with papery bracts is also useful in the carefree border, as it increases slowly and needs no attention: *Centaurea macrocephala* which grows to 5 feet in good soil, but is never so tall in mine. The leaves are long, hairy and rather pale green, but it is the flower buds that create interest—and covetousness on the part of flower arrangers! Each large round bud is covered with overlapping, crinkled bronze bracts. I was once showing the plant to visitors and said I did not know what *macrocephala* meant and a schoolgirl in the party put me right! It is, of course, 'big head'. When later the yellow flowers open from the buds I always feel it is somewhat an anti-climax.

Most of the campanulas increase rather fast, or seed themselves far more than one wants, but not *Campanula latifolia*, with its large hanging bells, which are beautifully shaped. The dark blue form *C. l.* Brantwood is very rich and sumptuous, more violet-purple in colour than blue, but the one I like best has pure white flowers and is attributed to Miss Willmott.

Of course the sedums are grown for autumn flowers, but they are evergreen and their foliage is useful all through the year. When the garden is coming to life in early May the different colours in sedum foliage are very distinct. There is a purple bloom on *S.* Ruby Glow, the delicate shades of cream and pale green of *S. spectabile variegatum* show up best in a shady place—but one has to look out for leaves that have gone back to green. The blue-grey of any ice plant, plum-coloured in the case of *S. maximum atropurpureum*, makes a lovely background for any bright colour. *S. telephium roseum* must receive its adulation early in the year before it loses its soft pink colouring or gets swamped by more luxuriant growth. Those early shoots look almost like wax, in a soft pink and have prettily waved edges.

I always think one gets as much fun from watching the various plants coming through the ground as in seeing them actually flower. The various hardy orchids one plants between other plants are all busily pushing through in April and there is great anxiety as to whether or not they will flower. The early purple orchis, *O. mascula*, always does and I always get flowers from *O. elata* if I can remember the last place where I have planted it. Years ago I wanted this very badly. It did not then seem to be in commerce and after worrying everyone I thought might help me I was eventually advised to write to a David Shackleton in Ireland. I had not met him then and I blush when I think of my crude approach but he took no offence and most generously dug up one of his precious plants.

I have never made up my mind where one should grow this. If it likes you it seems to increase wherever it is planted. It was growing in an ordinary bed when I saw it in David Shackleton's garden, and Mrs Anley does it superbly in light shade. I have tried it in a peat garden, in a garden of greensand under a north wall and in beds facing east. In none of these places has it really got going well, but perhaps it has not had a chance.

My first set-back came when I visited the late S. H. Walpole at Mount Usher. I had always heard about the magnificence of the Madeira orchid, *O. maderensis* (*O. foliosa*), marching beside one of the streams in the garden, and when he generously enquired if there was anything I would like, I asked for this orchid. Of course the compliment had to be returned and in reply to my offer he asked for *O. elata*. My one and only bulb had, therefore, to be brought to the surface and the small fry gently disentangled and replanted. I could repay his generosity only with the biggest bulb I had. These orchids are the easiest things to divide when they are doing well because the new plants are quite separate from the old one, and all that is necessary is to dig up the clump and separate the brittle tangled roots. I am sure this is the way the good growers do it and is no doubt the reason why the new plantings are without exception in a different place in the garden as the growers try to find the perfect spot.

I was given an orchis supposed to be Mr Bowles' Red, but which looks like an ordinary *O. mascula* to me. A kind Irish friend dug me a little crimson orchis from her garden and though it survives in greensand it does not increase and is not at all lavish with its flowers.

The other orchids come and go. I have bought *Cypripedium calceolus* many times but it does not flower well. To be honest I do not think it is an attractive flower, and if it was easy we would not bother with it, but no gardener can resist a challenge. *Epipactis palustris* does really well and runs about as I hoped the other would.

The handsome ribbed foliage of veratrums is at its best before the flowers appear. It has, of course, nothing to do with the flowers, but the time of year. These leaves have a fatal attraction for slugs and it is only when they first unfold that one can enjoy them without reservation, for very soon they are tattered and brown.

There is no plant better for a garden that is going to take care of itself, but they are plants that need a long time to get going. I often wonder if the magnificent clump of *Veratrum nigrum* in the garden at Tintinhull was put there when the garden was replanted in 1900. The clump at Newby Hall, near Ripon, is even bigger, and one of the most arresting sights in that exciting garden. One admires the tall spikes of black velvety flowers from a distance but they are also worth a close scrutiny, as each little bloom is a marvel of exquisite workmanship. In the white form *V. album*, delicate veining and soft shading adds to the beauty of shape and produces a flower that is certainly more off-white than pure white. For years I thought it was the green veratrum as it was labelled *V. viride* by mistake and the general effect is of grey-green. Then after some 10 to 15 years the green form deigned to flower and there was no mistaking its colour, which is bright emerald, as bright as young grass.

Quite different in colouring and outline *Perovskia atriplici-folia* is as graceful and arching as the other is straight and solid. But it is nearly as slow-growing as the veratrum and once planted should be left to grow. There are two forms, the ordinary one with plain leaves, and a better form with leaves cut at the edges. It is ironic that after waiting some 20 years for the ordinary one to become a sizeable clump I made the acquaintance of the better one and have to start all over again—but in a different place.

Gertrude Jekyll was right—as usual—when she grew *Sedum spectabile* under perovskia for its delicate tracery needs a solid contrast. There are better sedums since her day and now I have *S.* Autumn Joy under my perovskia on one side and *S. telephium* Munstead Red on the other side. As the stems of the perovskia become bleached in the winter, I never cut them down till the spring. They really are very white in the dark days, so white that one morning early visitors remarked how lovely the stems looked when white with hoar frost. I had to use great diplomacy in my reply. It happened to be a wet morning with no suggestion of frost.

A stalwart for year-to-year enjoyment is elecampane, *Inula helenium*. It is interesting from the moment its black-backed leaves appear and very handsome when in full flower, with very large leaves and big yellow daisy flowers. I must also mention the monardas for though they are surface rooting they go on for year after year if the ground is not too dry. I still think the bright crimson *Monarda* Cambridge Scarlet is the most satisfactory variety to grow.

The average michaelmas daisy spreads too fast for a 'leave it alone' border. Many of them seed, and if one is not careful it is easy to give hospitality to one that pushes out strong underground stems in all directions, stems which are shaggy with roots and which love to work through the roots and the rhizomes of iris. There are a few michaelmas daisies, however, that increase so slowly that they can be trusted in the most select company. I have to watch over *Aster lateriflorus horizontalis* to make sure it is still with me and when I am asked to part with a piece I have difficulty in getting off a scrap without ruining the plant. But it is worth the trouble for the tiny lavender flowers have crimson centres and stud the stems in a most un-aster-like way.

Many of the *amellus* type are slow to increase and never get out of hand. They vary in different gardens. Though the pale blue *A. a.* Lac de Geneve is almost embarrassing in the speed of its increase, such old favourites as *A. a.* King George in rich blue and Sonia in pink just peg along, and are vigorous enough to justify their place in the garden but no more. I was given up by *A. a.* Ultramarine years ago, and some of the others come and go. I enjoy an unnamed *amellus* that came from an old garden, and which may be the mother of them all, and two similar species are never invasive with me. *A. thomsonii* has smallish, rather pale flowers, and endears itself by its dignity and control. The one I have had for years is about 9 inches tall but I see the size is given as 2 feet in many nurserymen's lists, so mine must be the one they call *A. t. nanus*.

I think the taller type must have been used to produce *A. frikartii*, a hybrid between *A. amellus* and *A. thomsonii* and sometimes called 'The Wonder of Staffa'. It varies considerably and some of us are luckier than others. The best ones have large flowers of good deep blue (but never, I think, warrant the description 'peacock blue' which I have seen sometimes) and the centres should be orange. At Hidcote, the National Trust Garden in Gloucestershire, they have a beautiful form, and it is a joy to see it growing in profusion. I like it with the tall penstemon, Pennington Gem, with its small flowers of pale pink, or even the coral pink *P. isophyllus*.

Another aster that needs more than average protection is the old *A. tradescantii*, which can easily disappear in the winter when it has not much to show. I never cut mine down till spring, partly for this reason, but principally because the slender arching stems are lovely even when brown and dry.

Cimicifugas thrive in moist shady places but I find they do well in an ordinary flower bed that is not too sunny and is not particularly dry. Some people complain that they have rather an unpleasant smell, and one variety is in fact called *foetida*, but I have never noticed it. They undoubtedly have a repellent effect on some insects, and the colloquial name for the plant is Bugbane; the bugs they are reputed to frighten are in Siberia. But nothing detracts from the character of the plants, which have dignity as well as beauty.

There are many good things about *Kirengeshoma palmata* and one is its dignified and slow increase. All it asks is shade and lime-free soil, adequate moisture, and to be left alone. I always become very deaf when asked to chisel off bits from my plants. Although it does not flower till the autumn one can have fun watching it from the end of April. Then the new shoots are pushing through and the stems as they grow remind me of bamboos. They are smooth and green and have purplish markings where the leaves emerge. The leaves are beautiful, very sharply cut and in softest green. We get the flowers in autumn, small and waxy in soft yellow on dark stems.

One of the most graceful plants one can have—and sometimes the most exasperating—is that creature of many names, *Dierama pulcherrima*, which we used to call *Sparaxis pulcherrima*. Mostly it is referred to as the Wand-flower, but sometimes one hears it called Venus' Fishing Rod or Fairies' Fishing Rod. It does not take kindly to being moved and to try to divide it is a waste of time. The safest way to establish new plants is from small pot-grown

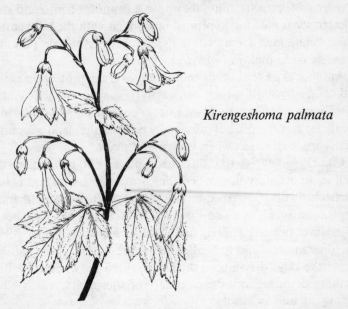

Kirengeshoma palmata

seedlings. Even then they will lose their foliage after being re-planted and it takes a year for the plant to become established. I wonder how many plants have been dug up while the newcomer is settling down below ground. It makes a great deal of seed and in some gardens quite a number of seedlings appear, but seldom where they are wanted. For the wand-flower needs placing in the garden. Its graceful stems can be 6 feet tall and are hung with flowers which can be shades varying from pink to white. It is lovely planted at the top of a bank, or above a wall, where its graceful outline can be enjoyed to the full. Sometimes it is a good idea to plant it at the end of a path, with one on each side so that they make an arch. Even before the flowers open the buds are beautiful, and when the plant is fully out and the exquisite flowers sway in the wind it is one of the loveliest sights in the garden.

A nursery in Northern Ireland specialises in dieramas and has produced a range of dwarf varieties which are sturdy and vigorous. These have been raised from a South African dwarf, deep-carmine-rose in colour, and from their best forms of *Dierama pulcherrima*.

CHAPTER THREE

Planting for Permanence

We all know the parts of our gardens that take care of themselves. They are the corners that give us no trouble, for they always look nice and go on for months on end without receiving attention of any kind.

There are beds furnished with herbaceous plants that come into this category but most of these carefree plantings have evergreen shrubs as a backbone. One place in my garden never shames me as I pass by; it is never crying out for staking, or deadheading and replanting, and is just as comforting in midwinter as in the middle of summer.

At the back is a large bush of *Juniperus media pfitzeriana*, which I planted as a screen when I fenced off a small part of the garden for the tenant living in the furnished end of my house. I needed a shield and was advised to plant this conifer, which makes a wide spreading bush with feathery branches. It lives up to its catalogue description of a slow grower for after more than 20 years it has not become uncomfortably big. In front on one side is a big bush of *Mahonia japonica*, which has thickened up with the years but has not become too corpulent. The only attention it needs—and gets—is the removal of the old flowering shoots and these I try to get off before the lovely blue berries form. Cutting as I do, at the roughened part of the stem about 6 inches down, two shoots are produced where before there was one, and so the bush becomes wider and more solid. As it does not grow upwards the juniper, which is slightly higher, keeps pace with it. On the other side of the conifer is a *Daphne retusa*, which flowers in May and June when the mahonia has at last come to the end of its long flowering season. There are herbaceous plants growing nearby, *Anthericum liliago* with its white flowers in late spring, and *Liriope spicata*, which has spikes of blue in September. Neither requires any attention, nor does the rock campanula, *C. portenschlagiana*, which fills in crevices in the paving and produces flowers all through the summer.

A border which also gives me no trouble is dominated by a purple-leaved filbert, *Corylus maxima purpurea*. It is underplanted with *Euonymus fortunei* Silver Queen, a neat little evergreen shrub which grows slowly and is always attractive. In the early months it shows up well, but by August there is so much foliage on the filbert that the euonymus is hidden. Large bushy plants of rue (*Ruta graveolens*) would be a better choice because they are big enough to show up against the nut and the two colours are very good for each other.

Against the permanent plants some easy herbaceous subjects give colour of a different kind. *Salvia verticillata* is used as ground cover but I do not think it is a very good choice because it soon grows too big and has to be cut back. *Phlox paniculata* in mauve and white gives less trouble. It is much taller than the ordinary type, takes up little room and stands up well between shrubs. Other plants that would look well and need no attention are *Asphodeline lutea*, flowering in May and *Galtonia candicans* in July or early August.

Another bed that gives me no work is dominated by *Rosa* Nevada. It makes a large informal bush, with pale foliage, and is almost thornless. Its flowers are creamy-white and turn pink as they age. Unlike many other shrub roses it goes on flowering most of the summer. Like most of the old fashioned or species roses it can look bare about the legs, and one is grateful for large, loose plants of euphorbia which grow in front. This euphorbia was given to me as *E. characias vivepara* because some of the florets turn to little shoots, very suitable for making new plants. It has enormous, rather loose heads of love-bird-green flowers which last for a long time. In front of the euphorbia some of the less usual bergenias do well. Most of them are the ones with rather small dark leaves such as *B. purpurascens* or *B. milesii*, which colour well in winter, making good colour contrast for the euphorbias.

A bed in the garden which I never have to worry about has a sprawling bush of *Lonicera nitida* Baggesen's Gold as a centrepiece. This golden form is much slower in growth than the green type and my plant has not doubled its size in 10 years. I never cut it and the only pruning it gets is when we cut off bits for cuttings. With it I grow the tall variegated form of the grass *Miscanthus sinensis*, and *Sedum maximum atropurpureum*, which is a good all-the-year-round plant. The early growth of the sedum is low but colourful and when, in late summer, the branching fleshy stems have large flower-heads of the same mahogany colour as the leaves the effect is very good. With strong-growing shrubs round it it needs little or no staking. *Artemisia pontica* and *Potentilla fruticosa farreri* complete the picture. The artemisia is a good grey—rather than silver—plant, with very straight spikes about 18 inches high. The foliage is fine and it increases steadily, though quite slowly, and may need a little cutting back from time to time. The potentilla flowers continuously all through the summer, and although it does not keep its leaves in winter the bare shoots of the shrub are not unpleasing.

Prostrate conifers are a great help in furnishing the garden for they need no attention at all until they have to be curtailed. A very good hard-wearing juniper for use at corners or for covering slopes or growing at the edge of stone paths is *Juniperus communis hornibrookii*. It has flat branches of grey-green foliage which pile on top of each other as the plant gets older. It associates very well with bergenias, especially the large-leaved *B. cordifolia* and any part of the garden so planted will look attractive all through the year. There will be flowers on the bergenia early in the year, and any other trouble-free plant can be grown with it to give colour later on. The orange *Geum borisii* flowers on and off over a long period and needs no staking, nor does the blue *Stokesia laevis*, commonly known as Stoke's Aster, and producing large blue flowers in August and September. It has exceptionally good foliage which is evergreen. *Dictamnus albus caucasicus* is dark plum colour when it has finished flowering and makes a good shape. The seed pods are covered with darker hairs and look more like burgeoning buds than empty pods.

Beside the old farm gate that leads into the barton I have more permanent planting. It is the lower end of the rock garden (made against a south-facing wall) and in the corner which has a south-west aspect there is a *Chimonanthus praecox luteus*, to give luxuriant glossy foliage in the summer months, and sparkling transparent yellow flowers in the winter. Near it the hardy fuchsia, Mrs Popple, makes a fine display in the summer. Beneath the chimonanthus the yellow-foliaged *Lonicera nitida* makes a sprawling informal bush, and on the wall behind is *L. tellmanniana*. This honeysuckle is very nearly evergreen. At the bottom level there are plants of *Bergenia ciliata* with great hairy leaves and long sprays of pink flowers so early in the year that they are often ruined by frost. A particularly good form of *Hydrangea macrophylla* (probably Altona) is also in the picture, with very large, very deep pink flowers.

A euphorbia put itself nearby—a seedling of *E. wulfenii*, with typical *wulfenii* flower heads but with the more compact build of *E. characias*. The best of the senecios for winter beauty is *S. Ramparts*, raised by Mrs Underwood of Colchester, and with it I grow the dwarf rose Little White Pet, which flowers most generously and needs little pruning. I take off the finished flower heads and that is all. Other evergreen plants are in this trouble-free planting: a variegated rue has leaves of cream and pale green which lighten a large bush of lavender close by. In the winter particularly I appreciate the golden form of Japanese honeysuckle, *Lonicera japonica aureo-reticulata*, which is supposed to be growing on the wall behind, and is to some extent, but some of it has got tired of climbing and has flung itself down on the south-facing bed below, to twine its way through the lavender and small shrubs and light up their sombreness. The honeysuckle is golden for most of the year but as the days get colder the leaves become soft old rose, and are really lovely. The gold of the climbing honeysuckle is picked up by the golden-foliaged *Lonicera* Baggesen's Gold, and also lightens rather a dark and dull little shrub which has its compactness as its main recommendation. *Spiraea bullata* is very slow growing. Its crimped leaves are very dark and it has rather small rose-crimson flowers in July and August. It was one of the first plants I grew from a cutting so it must have been sitting in its present position for 25 years and is still only about 18 inches high and 27 inches wide, but it is a very tightly packed little shrub which never needs any attention whatsoever.

A blue hyssop is pleasant in late August. I also grow hyssops in pink and white. They are neat, shrubby little plants that do best if cut back drastically after flowering and then can be left to their own devices. A good herbaceous plant to flower in late summer and autumn is *Geranium wallichianum* Buxton's Blue. By the end of the season it will have made a very big plant, studded with blue flowers, which have conspicuous white centres. After the flowers are over, or even before they are over, the leaves colour beautifully and are a joy for many weeks. It grows from a single crown so has to be increased by root cuttings or from seed—I do not find it seeds itself to any extent so it is not a nuisance.

When I plan my garden I try always to have enough evergreen plants to make an attractive structure throughout the year and tend to think more about the winter than the summer, because the summer really looks after itself. But not all gardeners feel the same way. Some people do not go out in the garden in the winter, or the garden may be some way from the house and so is not seen from the house, and in such a case one can use permanent plants which are attractive only in the summer. I was much impressed by some of the plantings in the National Trust Garden of Crathes Castle, in Kincardineshire, because many of the beds need very little attention for weeks on end. One in particular was especially happy when I saw it in July and it seemed to me it would go on looking happy for a very long time.

A large bush of *Paeonia lutea ludlowii* made a magnificent light green background among trees. In front the purple weigela, *W. florida foliis purpureis*, showed up extremely well and I wondered why we so seldom see this weigela, with its rich dark leaves. In front of the weigela huge clumps of *Alchemilla mollis* had billowing mounds of tiny green flowers and made a wonderful contrast. There were clumps of hemerocallis, with pale orange and greeny-yellow flowers, and huge clumps of hostas, with large leaves and lilac flowers in late summer. There were no garish colours to distract, and nothing needed staking, but the contrast of different coloured foliage and flowers in soft pale shades made a picture as lovely as any I have seen in any garden.

There are many such schemes that can be worked out, and where possible the clumps should be fairly large so that one gets a generous effect, and then planted as close together as one can to avoid weeds appearing between them.

CHAPTER FOUR

Gardens without Grass

If there is no grass in the garden one's worries practically disappear, because it is the lawns in the garden that are the great worry when labour is short. It does not matter if the flower beds are left for a week or two but grass must be cut regularly if any enjoyment at all is to be had from the rest of the garden. No one will deny that good grass makes a garden and, equally, bad grass ruins a garden. Nothing shows up the beauty of flowers and shrubs so well as grass—it rests the eye and gives a feeling of peace and satisfaction. But it becomes an eyesore if it is allowed to get out of hand. It must be cut regularly and the edges must be trimmed every time the grass is cut.

There are many reasons why it is difficult to get the grass cut. Labour, of course, is the main problem, and those of us who rely on casual labour are the worst sufferers. I can remember one period of my gardening life when I had a very nice girl to do my grass. She did it exceptionally well because she had a knack with machinery and the mower knew it. Get an unmechanical person to do the grass and everything goes wrong, the mower stalls, washers and nuts fall off, and there is endless trouble. The trouble, of course, was that my treasure did not come when I expected her. I know it was not her fault because she had many other things to do but I can remember the disappointment as time after time I came back to find the grass still uncut.

Then there are weather hazards. With a full-time gardener it does not matter if it rains one day but when one has a gardener one day a week that is inevitably the day it rains. It is the same for the weekend gardener. Some years it rains every weekend and the grass has to be left two and sometimes three weeks.

Gardeners who like to do all their own gardening are at a great disadvantage if they become unable to cut the grass, and I know several crippled gardeners who have designed their gardens without grass so that they can still take care of them. Such gardens need not look too cold or bare if plenty of foliage is grown at ground level, and with small gardens particularly this has distinct advantages. We all know how plants in a border that is next to grass have to be set well back to be kept out of the way of the mower, and when space is limited there is no room for mowing stones or other barriers between grass and flower bed. The edge of the grass becomes very defined, almost prim in its straightness—or curves if one is very dashing and goes in for an oval or circle of grass. The planting looks formal even if it is not, because there is this area of bare soil next to the grass, whereas, if the garden is paved instead of grassed the picture is quite different.

One of the great advantages of paving is that one can plant right up to its edge so that half of the plant sprawls over the stone. Most plants appreciate a cool root run and the nepetas, gypsophilas, teucriums and bergenias planted in this way usually do remarkably well.

And just think of the valuable space that is saved in the flower bed. Owners of small gardens are so often frustrated because they would like to grow so many more things than they have room for, and with paving instead of grass they can. It does not matter so much to owners of big gardens—although no keen gardener ever has enough room—so I do not think paving is the answer when the garden is very large. Enormous tracts of paving would be difficult to bring to life as a green and restful garden but in small areas it works well.

Dwarf shrubs with an informal habit are very useful at the edge of the paving so long as they do not get too tall. The silver senecio, *S. laxifolius*, grows big in time but usually does its increasing sideways and with judicial pruning can be kept in bounds. *Cotinus coggygria*, the Smoke Bush, is good for an occasional mound of foliage either in green or crimson. I have never made up my mind which form I like best. The purple form, *Cotinus coggyria foliis purpureis*—to give it its newest name—is the one usually grown, but there are others. *C. c. Royal Purple* has good dark coloured leaves, especially striking in bright sun after rain. The deep wine-red leaves of *C. c. rubrifolius* seem to be translucent with the sun behind them. Another choice is *C. c. atropurpureus*, which has green leaves and large panicles that billow like pink smoke. *C. c. Flame* is the best green-leaved form for autumn colour.

These shrubs will grow big in time so must be planted where a large mound of foliage will help the scheme. The fleshy *Euphorbia myrsinites* would look well with the purple-leaved rhus. With the green-leaved variety a dwarf sedum such as *S. Ruby Glow* would be effective. This makes tight clumps and the flower stems usually grow near the ground.

Most of us grow small plants in crevices in paving, and when paving takes the place of grass the plants chosen should be those that are inclined to spread on top of the stone. Many plants grow very happily between stones, particularly if they are started off well with good soil, then firmly planted and well watered in. Creeping thymes—*Thymus serpyllum*—make very wide mats and cover a good area. The colour of the stone used can make a difference to the variety of thyme chosen. On a very light stone the golden variety shows up well. Stones with a pinkish tinge make a good background for the grey, woolly thyme, *T. s. lanuginosus*, the bright green leaves of *T. s. albus* look well with blue stone, and the honey-coloured Bath or Ham Hill stone, which looks well with anything, is particularly attractive when *T. Annie Hall* grows on it. This thyme has tiny, very bright green leaves.

Even lighter in colour is the delicate foliage of *Phuopsis stylosa*. This plant has one long root and throws out its ruffled stems in all directions, some about a foot long, with small pink flowers at the end of each. Rock phloxes spread, too, from a single root and so do such plants as *Silene schafta* and armerias. The best little plant for covering stone with a film of minute foliage is *Arenaria balearica* but it needs a shady, damp spot to get started. It could be planted in the shade of one of the taller plants that may be used at the edge of the paving, and when well established will creep out into the open.

The various forms of *Saxifraga umbrosa* will spread in all directions and make quite heavy mats in time. I have plantings over a yard square in my garden, all growing on top of stone. The variations of this useful plant are worth considering. The form known as *variegata* or *aurea* is glinted with gold and has crimson shadings in winter. *S. geum* is very dark green with deeply scalloped leaves, which turn bright crimson in autumn and grow on long stalks. The form *S. g.* Inglesborough has even deeper indentations on the leaves. *S. u. primuloides* is a small version of the ordinary London Pride and the form named Elliott's Variety (collected by Clarence Elliott) is more compact with deeper-coloured flowers.

Sometimes bigger crevices are needed to take mossy saxifrages, and chamomile—*Anthemis nobilis*. *Mentha pulegium* (Pennyroyal) also needs a big space so that it makes a large patch of green.

Experiments have proved that few plants can be used to take the place of grass when it is a question of hard wear, but small lawns that are not on a direct route give welcome patches of green. We often hear about chamomile lawns but they are not as easy to keep as some of the enthusiasts would have us believe. The form of *Anthemis nobilis* called Treneague is the best to use because it does not flower. But it is rather billowy in growth and does not begin to compare with the billiard-table smoothness of real turf. It is a good bright green and smells deliciously of apples. Also aromatic are the various creeping thymes which make a pleasant, patch if the different varieties are grown together. They need shearing after flowering. Saginas can be used in the same way. *Sagina pilifera* has short grassy foliage which smells mildly of violets. It spreads fairly fast but is not hardwearing enough for big areas. *S. p. aurea* is the golden version, but this, I think, should be used in paving crevices rather than as a lawn, because it is green we want to take the place of grass, not golden foliage.

A paved garden can be quite attractive if enough foliage is introduced. I once visited a big garden with the usual lawns, shrubberies and herbaceous borders and as we passed through an iron gate my hostess said to me 'And this is my leisure garden'. It was a walled garden with narrow beds under the walls. These were wide enough to take the many creepers that covered the walls, but were not otherwise heavily planted. The rest of the garden was paved, and the paving had been laid in concrete so that there were no cracks between the stones. The beds in the garden were arranged in a formal design and were absolutely crammed with plants that needed little attention. Hardy geraniums, silver plants of the santolina, senecio and helichrysum persuasion, evergreen iberis and *Teucrium chamaedrys* were growing together so that no soil was visible and the plants were spilling over the stone in all directions, giving an air of abundance and informality. There were several trees in the garden, cherries and a catalpa, and under them were hellebores and evergreen plants. *Euphorbia robbiae* is excellent for such a position and the mildly creeping *Mahonia aquifolium*, which has glossy foliage often crimson in spring. There were several seats in the garden in sun and shade, for in this garden one could sit and rest without the constant worry of seeing jobs that had to be done. The garden did not look cold or bare and was attractive at any month in the year.

Gardens without grass mean gardens with no grass at all so something else has to be used to divide borders from paths and in other places where strips of grass are usually grown. A border of the large-leaved *Bergenia cordifolia* can be very attractive, particularly in autumn and winter when the great shiny leaves turn red, and in the spring when there are pink or white flowers. The dark-leaved *Geum borisii* is evergreen and though they may clash with other flowers in the border the dark orange flowers are attractive and show up well under trees. The glossy leaves of *Veronica gentianoides* also make a firm evergreen border. This veronica has pale blue flowers on long stalks which can be sheared off after flowering. The ubiquitous London Pride, *Saxifraga umbrosa*, makes a good border for rose beds, and *Alchemilla mollis* (although not evergreen) has solid tough roots and is substantial enough to grow in front of a hedge. At Inverewe, the

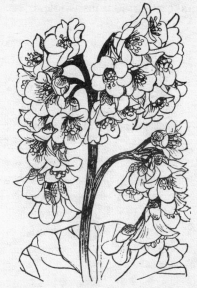

Bergenia cordifolia

National Trust Garden in Scotland, one path is edged on each side with *Peltiphyllum peltatum*. Though not evergreen the roots make solid mats with large pink flowers in April, and later, large leaves which turn crimson in autumn. I have heard the autumn display at Inverewe likened to a butcher's shop!

A big garden without grass is more difficult to plan but use can be made of the natural beauties. We appreciate the value of the trees, and if there is moss under them it can be left as an informal lawn. It needs brushing when leaves are falling and this keeps it in good condition.

If there is no moss rough grass can be left and the garden planted on woodland lines. A path will have to be cut several times a year, but this is not nearly so arduous as cutting grass regularly every week.

The garden without grass needs more careful planting than one on the usual lines. It can easily become cold and hard, but need not be if softening influences are used to the full. Paving in warmer tones is easier than the colder 'blue' stone. Very happy effects are made by using stones of softer shades together so that they make a harmonious whole.

CHAPTER FIVE

Rock Gardening the Easy Way

We all know that a rock garden is the most difficult part of a garden to keep well, if it is to be run on regular lines, with many small and precious plants which have to be maintained without encroachment by more vigorous neighbours. Most rock plants need special treatment—they often require different soil and certainly like sharp drainage, and dedicated rock gardeners usually cover the soil with chippings, which have to be renewed from time to time, and always must be kept free of weeds. If a bad weed gets into a rock garden often the whole garden has to be remade to eradicate such enemies as couch grass and bindweed, which delve under rocks and work through the roots of precious plants. In fact to keep an average rock garden in perfect condition means endless weeding as well as regular cutting back and trimming.

In a carefree garden I think the only way to grow one's tiny treasures is in troughs, and to allow other, more free-growing, plants to furnish the rock garden. Not perhaps aubrieta, alyssum and arabis, which are happy in walls and at the edge of beds, but plants which will, in time, cover a fair amount of space and will merge pleasantly with other things to make a happy blending of colour.

Rock phloxes and rock roses need only to be trimmed after flowering. There are veronicas such as *V. peduncularis* Nyman's Variety, and *V. pectinata rosea* that make big mats in a reasonable time. I have not been lucky with *Dryas octopetala* of recent years, although I once had a three-tier plant at the front of my rock garden. I think it likes a neutral or acid soil and should be started off with plenty of peat if the soil has a high lime content.

It keeps close to the ground in a flat mat and its small oak-shaped leaves are neat and evergreen. After the white flowers on 4-inch stems are over, there will be silky seed heads to persist for many weeks. Wherever it is planted it should be given space to grow; if it does well it will work its way down over stones and flat beds to the lowest level. It flowers from May to July and the seed heads last a long time after that.

Another rock plant that behaves in the same way is *Polygonum vaccinifolium*, and this, too, seems happier in acid or neutral soil, although it will succeed in limy soil if started off well and left alone. I had trouble in establishing it in the beginning because I did not leave it alone. When people asked me for a bit I pulled pieces off and thought that because they were furnished with wisps of root they would soon settle down in a new place and the parent plant would not notice, but would soon produce more growth to take their place. It did not work out like that and now I leave it alone.

A good dwarf perennial candytuft that will provide white flowers in May on dark evergreen foliage is *Iberis sempervirens* Little Gem. Less rampant campanulas are good, *C. garganica* is neat, with well-cut leaves, and produces light blue flowers for most of the summer. *C.* Norman Grove has violet bells and *C. planiflora alba* produces sturdy little white spikes about 6 inches high, with very dark foliage.

In a big rock garden the *carpatica* campanulas stand up well. I still think the old *C. c.* Isobel is one of the best with wide, saucer-shaped flowers in violet-blue, and for a white, *C. c.* Bressingham White is a good one to choose.

The geranium I should pick would be *G.* Russell Prichard, which makes a rosette of silver foliage and endless magenta-pink flowers on long trails. For late summer and autumn G. *wallichianum* Buxton's Blue makes a handsome clump, with white-centred blue flowers and leaves that colour well.

Also late flowering, *Convolvulus mauritanicus* can become quite a big plant after a few years. It is not hardy everywhere and it often helps to plant the root under the protection of a stone.

Another rather generous plant which takes care of itself is *Ceratostigma plumbaginoides*. If possible it should be wedged between stones so that its roots cannot escape, and in self-defence it has to concentrate on flowering.

Small shrubs are labour-saving; *Hebe macrantha* has very large white flowers and close-packed leaves and in a very sheltered spot *H. hulkeana* is well worth trying. It has very beautiful glossy leaves and sprays of lavender flowers. It is sometimes possible to keep this New Zealand shrub if it is protected by other shrubs. The spiraeas include some neat little plants that grow quite slowly and flower for most of the summer. The compact *S. bullata* grows to about 12 inches and has dark pink flowers and crinkled foliage. For a shady position the dwarf *Sorbus reducta* has mildly running roots and shaded pinkish-crimson berries.

For full sun the silver-foliaged *Euryops evansii* makes a neat little bush that looks almost white. It needs regular trimming otherwise it can become leggy. *Dorycnium hirsutum*, on the other hand, forms a low spreading bush of soft grey foliage and small pink pea flowers. In some gardens it seeds itself quite freely, and this often happens in gardens by the sea.

It is quite safe to plant small bulbs among these permanent plants. I grow *Brodiaea laxa* in full sun but in one garden I know it grows well and flowers freely under trees. Its violet-purple flowers are attractive in late summer. Colchicums also flower at the end of the summer and come up year after year.

A lot depends on the size of the rock garden but if it is big and if there is room against stones facing south nerines flower for several weeks, and small pockets filled with sternbergias are always cheerful. *S. lutea* is the form usually grown but some people think that *S. lutea augustifolia*, with narrower leaves, has the better flowers.

The little snowdrop that flowers in the autumn is often planted in sun. *Galanthus nivalis olgae* flowers well when established and is exciting to find in late October and early November.

Most of us grow hardy cyclamen under trees and hedges but

there is no reason really why they should not be grown in the rock garden as well.

I even grow a few rather special dwarf ivies in my rock garden because I know that there they are safe. The variegated form of *Hedera helix sagittifolia* is small and elegant and so is another small variegated ivy, *H. h.* Heisse.

CHAPTER SIX

Making the Most of Walls

Gardeners with walls can get much of their work done for them as there are many climbing plants that look after themselves and are quite happy clambering over other plants.

It is worth getting one's walls properly wired in the first place. Vine 'eyes' are usually easy to hammer into mortar and if a new wall is being built it is a good scheme to have the eyes (or staples if preferred) put in the mortar before it sets. The idea is to run horizontal wires, about 12 or 18 inches apart, along the length of the wall so that there is a permanent structure on which to train the first selection of wall plants.

Some people use trellis, either wooden or plastic, and this is quite easy, but I always think it is a little too visible and I prefer wires on a beautiful old wall. Perhaps one should say here 'husbands permitting', for some husbands have a strong feeling about anything that can harm the fabric, and some will not allow anything to grow on house walls. Ivy can be destructive if it is allowed to get a firm hold on a wall, although I do not think it does any harm to trees. Valerian is another enemy of walls. The tiny seedlings grow in wall crevices and one thinks how pretty they are and that this is a good way of dealing with valerian, which seeds itself far too liberally when it gets into a garden. But valerian roots get very big in time and stone and mortar are no match for them, so that eventually the wall has to be rebuilt.

At the east end of my small front garden I have a fine *Mahonia aquifolium* growing in the wall. It was there when we bought the house, and it makes a wonderful screen against the road and a good background for the hellebores, hydrangeas,

white daffodils and leucojums that grow in the bed in front. I
try to keep the mahonia to the wall and do not allow it to come
out into the bed, but I know in time it will finish off the wall.

In the meantime I enjoy its glossy evergreen leaves and cut
little bits off the new crimson shoots in early spring. A peach-
coloured chaenomeles is growing in the corner and a plant of
nepeta sowed itself in a chink on top of the wall. Most people
would think there was enough crammed into this small space,
but I am always greedy, and I put the white clematis Marie
Boisselot into the corner made by the walls; now its large, flat,
white flowers adorn the mahonia and the chaenomeles and
swarm over the nepeta to make layered festoons on the outside
of the walls. This clematis has white stamens, as well as its long
white petals, and flowers from May to December in my garden.

The dark red *Rosa* Guinée, which has velvety flowers and very
good hips, has the next bit of wall. So far Marie Boisselot has
not reached it nor has *Clematis* White Moth—a form of *alpina*—
which is playing about near the gate, climbing through another
chaenomeles—flame-coloured this time—and enjoying the shade
of a large *Hydrangea villosa*.

Honeysuckles are among the easiest wall plants to grow. They
find their own support, and if one chooses one of the evergreen
types they clothe the area where they are growing. *Lonicera
japonica halliana* is a most obliging plant. It is practically evergreen and has a very strong scent. The flowers are more concentrated on the stems than in some of the honeysuckles; they
open white and change to yellow as they age. My other favourite is *L. tellmanniana*, which is one of the highest growing honeysuckles. It has coppery-orange flowers and fresh green leaves,
and though not evergreen the foliage lasts a long time. If only it
was scented it would be perfect. The Belgian form of our hedge-
row honeysuckle, *L. periclymenum belgica*, has very dark leaves
and flowers flushed on the outside with red-purple. It is known
as Early Dutch, and *L. p. serotina* is called Late Dutch. This
variety also has flowers flushed on the outside with red-purple,
and has the same rather dark leaves.

The very useful qualities that make these honeysuckles so valuable can sometimes be a problem. If there is a small tree or bush growing against the wall the honeysuckle will transfer its embracing stems from the support it has found on the wall to the unsuspecting plant. I have a young *Sorbus vilmorinii* planted against my boundary wall and it still has the slenderness of youth. *Lonicera japonica halliana* had managed to wind itself a long way up the tree before I noticed it. Though so young the sorbus had its first good crop of pink-flushed fruits that year, and even if not choked its beauty would have been ruined.

Jasmines can also take care of themselves and are clever at finding any wire or nail for support. Left to themselves they make a very luxuriant cover for a wall or building but only *Jasminum primulinum* can be considered evergreen. There is no need to waste a warm wall on jasmines; they do not appear to notice what aspect they are given and are splendid plants for north walls. *J. officinale* has the most generous nature, and goes on producing its scented white flowers until late November. I have a silver-variegated form of this—also on a north wall—but so far it has not flowered. I gave away my plant of *J. officinale affine* because it made so much growth that it was difficult to find the pink-flushed flowers, but I would not turn out the form which has gold variegations on the leaves. I do not think it grows so luxuriantly as the unvariegated form; certainly the flowers are not hidden. These two variegated varieties—gold and silver—share a north wall and have pushed their way under the guttering and are exploring the roof above. The golden one is now competing with a less exuberant chaenomeles and *J. officinale* has reached the place where a variegated ivy is growing, but the ivy hugs the wall, and the jasmine is exploring everything it can reach from the wires which are some distance from the wall.

The ivies I use to give me interest in the winter are the large-leaved ones: *Hedera canariensis* Gloire de Marengo (*H. c. variegata*) can be dazzlingly white, with its variegation of silver, grey-green and touches of pink, but it can also be rather dark at times and *H. colchica dentata variegata*, which is variegated with rich cream (or pale yellow), has a brighter effect and brings sunshine into the winter garden. I use it in a dark north-east corner with golden privet (*Ligustrum ovalifolium aureo-marginatum*) to give a better view from the house. Another jasmine, which has small golden-variegated leaves and pink flowers, grows here, and this is host to *Clematis* Hagley Hybrid, with its rich pink flowers. As *Garrya elliptica* does its flowering in the winter, I hope in time the clematis will use it as a background during the summer. A shell-pink China rose is already doing this on the other side, and it is exciting to find the delicate pink flowers among the grey-green leaves of the garrya. China roses are obliging creatures as they seem to like growing on a north wall and they flower on and off all the time, with a final burst of glorious bloom late in the autumn. I know my rose will make a fine show in October and November, and in very mild weather I have found flowers at Christmas time.

Members of the vine family make themselves very much at home wherever they happen to be, and are equipped with tendrils that wave about until they find something to which to attach themselves. They will make use of other plants if they are near enough for the tendrils to reach. I have a good example of this which I can see very easily out of my bedroom window. I planted a *Vitis* Miller's Burgundy on the front of the house because the powdered grey-green leaves look lovely against the honey-coloured stone of the house. This vine grows very luxuriantly and does not keep to the strands of wire I have given it below my window. It rears its strong stems well above the windows and would completely cover them if allowed. And as the vine comes into my vision I see the questing tendrils waving in the breeze seeking the support that is not there. A little farther along the wall they find the sturdy stems of the old rose Mme Caroline Testout and clutch her eagerly. The stems of this rose are often rather bare and the leaves of the vine make a lovely setting for the pink cabbage roses.

Another vine that makes use of any support it can find is *Vitis heterophylla*, more correctly called *Ampelopsis brevipedunculata*.

It has dark leaves, which are often nicely cut, and grows rapidly. I have never noticed its flowers but look hopefully in late summer for the blue berries I hope it will produce. They come in small clusters and are porcelain blue with tiny black spots. We usually blame the season if there are not many berries, but I understand if the root system is restricted there is more hope of a good crop.

The most vigorous vine I grow is *V. coignetiae*, a Japanese plant, with great heart-shaped leaves, rather rough in texture, which turn dazzling colours in the autumn. No wonder it can clamber to the top of tall trees if desired, for it is equipped with the longest, strongest tendrils I have ever seen. They are as tough as wire and once they find a support they take a muscular grip that is hard to disentangle. I let it ramble over roses on a fence and as it wanders far and wide it does not swamp any particular plant. I would not let it loose on my more frail treasures for it does not know restraint.

The purple-foliaged *Vitis vinifera purpurea* is not nearly so possessive. It has rich purple foliage, powdered with white meal in its early stages, and has black grapes.

CHAPTER SEVEN

Grass and Trees

It takes a strong-minded gardener to eschew all the delights of borders and rock gardens and find contentment in a landscape garden. To do this one must be sure that the grass will be cut regularly. Beyond that the garden will take care of itself most of the time.

One would not think that the setting we connect with stately homes would be just as good with a modern bungalow. But the fact is that this simple type of garden is just right for our modern small houses. The usual straight path, regular beds and neat hedges turn the place into a doll's house, with a prim look that is difficult to disguise, but a few trees and an unbroken sweep of grass give an air of mystery.

I remember visiting a garden of this type and arriving late in the evening. This particular garden was big in proportion to the bungalow, although that was large by ordinary standards, and as I drove up the path I saw trees by the light of my head-lamps. Flowers were growing round them in the grass, and I remember how lovely the red tulips looked in the night.

The garden had, in fact, been made before the house was built, so some of the trees were quite large. All were particularly good and interesting specimens, chosen by experts, and in this setting they could be seen and appreciated properly.

Round every tree were bulbs in the grass and I noticed how much more natural the trees looked growing this way than if little beds had been made. If the ground is well prepared and the tree planted in a very large hole, with reversed turves at the bottom, and then filled up with good soil, they get off to a good start and should not need further attention, but old manure can be used as a mulch and bonemeal administered in holes made by a crowbar.

The size and shape of the garden governs what trees and shrubs are used and how they are planted. All kinds of trees can be chosen; those that are evergreen and attractive all through the year, and flowering trees that give colour at different times. Sometimes a good effect can be made by grouping several trees together. I always slow down when I pass the arboretum at Westonbirt in Gloucestershire, to enjoy the tall golden conifers that are planted as a group. Whatever the time of year they look beautiful, and particularly so in winter, when the gold seems brighter and the effect more dazzling. Of course smaller trees must be used in a small garden. An occasional tree with variegated foliage makes a pleasant contrast, as do subjects good for autumn colour, such as *Euonymus alatus* for chalky soils and liquidambar for deep acid soils.

On the whole for a garden of this type trees are better than shrubs, because of cutting the grass round them, and because the planting should not in any way resemble a shrubbery. Most people would prefer a proper path through the garden, a path made carefully and treated with a bituminous substance and then gravelled, which would last indefinitely and require no weeding. An occasional shrub near this path seems in keeping, and foliage in different colours might well be considered. The purple-leaved sumach, *Cotinus coggygria foliis purpureis* is lovely, but I often wonder if the Smoke Bush—the form with green leaves and feathery grey inflorescences—is not even more beautiful. Laurustinus (*Viburnum tinus*) is a remarkably beautiful plant when allowed to grow naturally and has the advantage of being a winter-flowerer. Shape as well as colour is important, as it would be easy to make such a garden spotty, and great thought has to be given to the siting of the trees.

The garden I am thinking of had a few extras which undoubtedly made work and could be left out by gardeners who wanted to keep work to a minimum. In front of the house there was a small water and rock garden with a bridge, a weeping tree and primulas and iris by the water. The rock garden was not elaborate and the plants used were easy ones, but every gardener knows that a rock garden does require a good deal of work.

I think the small paved gardens at the back of the house would be more labour-saving. They were skilfully sited to one side or the other so that there was a good background of trees, and they seemed to fit into the scheme as if they belonged.

In several other places large troughs had been raised on stones and placed so that they had behind them a background of foliage, and in the paved gardens troughs were also a feature. I remember one of these gardens was on a slightly higher level and was approached by shallow steps, and the area of paving was rather irregular with a low wall and the troughs. Dwarf informal shrubs were used beside the steps and against the stone at the back so that the effect was softened and in keeping with the rest of the garden. The troughs were planted to give colour at different times of the year and were in harmony, whereas small beds planted with small subjects would have seemed quite out of keeping.

Another concession to normal gardening was a lavish display of pelargoniums and other bedding plants round the house. This definitely made a great deal of work, for the plants had to be raised and the beds replanted each year, but it achieved colour throughout the season. More labour-saving would be a wide border filled with easy evergreen shrubs that would make a permanently attractive planting, with perhaps a few easy perennials planted among them and bulbous plants such as *Iris unguicularis* (*I. stylosa*) and nerines against a south wall, but it would not be so colourful.

There is another type of natural garden that needs even less work, but it is only for those who live on the edge of a moor and very few of us do that. I have seen really most attractive gardens made from the natural terrain, with heathers and sometimes bilberries (*Vaccinium myrtillus*). The grass is usually close cropped, there may be boulders, and with luck a few trees. How often we walk over moorland and think how pleasant it would be to walk out from our houses into a natural garden; moor dwellers who have such a landscape at their door are wise to accept it as a gift from Heaven and not bring an artificial atmosphere into the scene. A fenced-in garden with a formal lay-out looks quite wrong in such a setting. A fence would keep out the animals, but it is the rabbits and sheep that crop the grass, and keep it fine and close. If one grows vegetables or any cultivated plant, they would eat them too but the natural moorland plants are safe when there is grass.

A little tidying up would no doubt be necessary in the beginning, and a clearance for a path, which would look best made of the natural outcrop. If there are no trees, a few silver birches or a Scots pine would look right in such a setting. The natural rock garden could be made by rearranging the boulders already on the site, but only the most ordinary and easy plants should be grown, plants that might be found in that kind of setting and which could be easily replaced if they were nibbled with the grass. *Dryas octopetala* would be a good choice, *Rubus arcticus* is easy and rewarding in acid soil, and also such plants as bearberry, *Arctostaphylos uva-ursi*, and cranberry, *Vaccinium oxycoccus*.

CHAPTER EIGHT

Nature's Largesse

One way to furnish the carefree garden is to leave some of the self-sown seedlings which nature distributes so lavishly. In any garden that is well filled with the natural type of plant—species rather than hybrids—a large number of seedlings come up year after year. I rely on many of them to help fill the garden, and am grateful for this source of treasure. Of course it means that you never use a hoe, except in the vegetable garden, but I never want to use a hoe and I would not let anyone hoe in my garden. This was always a little matter of argument when my husband was alive. He realised that hoeing was a quick way of keeping the garden free of weeds, and used to demonstrate how easy it was to reach the distant parts of the flower beds with a hoe. I had to watch silently while he sliced off everything in sight, small plants as well as weeds, but I was never dutiful enough to adopt the advice given me.

It is uncanny how often seedlings of plants appear that have not been grown in the garden for years. I bought a Fishbone Thistle, *Cirsium diacantha*, about 20 years ago. It is a biennial and I did not save seed. But about six years ago a little silver starfish of a plant appeared and I realised what it was. I rescued it from under the big clump of phlox which would have stifled it and it grew to maturity, which means a 2-foot slender thistle, with silvered leaves and small purple flowers. Since then I get three or four little plants every year, and if I have time I plant them together to make a feature. The Virgin's Milk Thistle, *Silybum marianum*, behaves in exactly the same way, but it makes a much bigger rosette and must be given about a square yard of space. Both these thistles are really more beautiful before the flower stalks appear; the Milk Thistle in particular has enormous leaves in its early stages, angular and bright green, and with conspicuous white veins which make a pattern. These are supposed to have been caused by drops of the Virgin's milk.

Large beds where I grow hellebores would be completely filled with self-sown plants if I allowed all of them to remain. I do not touch the beds much in the summer, and before I divide the hellebores—species and different types of *Helleborus orientalis*—there is a certain amount of bare space where the plants can develop quietly without disturbance. The bed is under old apple trees, in slight shade, and clumps of cultivated grass give height among the hellebores; bergenias are planted against the path.

Some of the strangers are massive. One year I had a 14-foot *Onopordon acanthium* and a huge clump of *Salvia sclarea turkestanica*, both of which had to be supported. I grow a luscious double pink opium poppy, which looks like a Malmaison carnation, and that seeds itself well. But not all the seedlings are true, and some are entrancing shades of lavender, mulberry and cerise. Some are double and others are single.

Anyone who has naturalised *Geranium pratense* in grass, which is the best place to grow it, knows what delightful colour breaks appear in the seedlings. Soft pinks, off-whites, greyish-white and every shade of blue appear, and when a pale, sad, pink geranium puts itself beside a faded lilac poppy the colour scheme is better than any man-made concoction.

Astrantia major is an inveterate seeder, but the solid clumps are never in the way, and the lacy flowers in white and pale green mix with everything. *A. biebersteinii* has more pink in its flowers and that seeds just as generously. And so does *A. carniolica*, which is much like *A. major* but usually more dwarf. Though the double meadow sweet (*Filipendula ulmaria fl. pl.*) sows itself in a mild way it is never an embarrassment. Its cut foliage and creamy-white flowers fit in anywhere. *Polemonium caeruleum* puts itself just where a touch of blue is needed, and campanulas add white or blue. *C. persicifolia* goes on flowering

for months on end, and *C. lactiflora* would give a second display if one cut off its finished flowers. Sometimes I find a stray
C. glomerata to make welcome contrast with deep blue. A
brighter blue is supplied by Love-in-the-Mist, *Nigella damas-
cena.*

I try not to be sentimental about *Atriplex hortensis*, which I
bought as Red Mountain Orach about 25 years ago. I have
never sown it since but every year there are more and more of
the little crimson seedlings. They look so harmless when they
appear, but leave them and they become towering 6-footers.
No one can deny that they are very beautiful and give rich
colour wherever they grow. In late afternoon, when the sun
shines through those handsome leaves they glow like rubies and
beautiful pictures can be made with them. The blue-green of
Euphorbia characias or *wulfenii* makes a wonderful foil, and if
these spurges do not sow themselves next to an atriplex the
Caper Spurge, *E. lathyrus*, most surely will.

This is as handsome a plant as anything in the garden, with
its grey-green leaves growing regularly at right angles. It lasts
well in water and is most attractive when the plant starts to
flower. The seeds look just like capers and can easily be taken
for them by the uninitiated, but as they are very poisonous it
is lucky that not many people are taken in. When the seeds are
ripe they burst with a noise like a miniature gun and drive the
gardener frantic because he knows that every seed means
another caper spurge, and it seems awful to pull out such
attractive plants by the hundred. Whatever one's resolutions
there are always plenty of *Euphorbia lathyrus* to grow with
atriplex.

Instead of a glaucous foil, a big clump of silver foliage looks
most handsome with atriplex with a backing of a conifer such as
Chamaecyparis lawsoniana fletcheri. The tobacco plant with
small green flowers, *Nicotiana rustica*, is also good with atriplex
and is a generous seeder.

Not all the plants that sow themselves are in the giant class.
Welsh poppies, *Meconopsis cambrica*, are really very pretty little

things, and those gardeners for whom they will not grow envy
me my hundreds. I am not always so enthusiastic because they
put themselves in the middle of more precious plants and infest
special beds I have made for rare bulbs. But when they intermingle their yellow or orange flowers with Mr Bowles' golden
grass, *Milium effusum aureum*, or pose in front of *Alchemilla
mollis* or *Euphorbia cyparissias*, I am grateful for their persistent
ways. If I had time I would collect the stragglers and replant
them together in a dark corner or under a wall, but that I know
I never shall be able to do, so I shall continue to put up with
their casual behaviour and appreciate the happy look they give
to the garden. After they are over we pull them by their hundreds
and yet I get more and more every year.

I would like the violets that sow themselves better if I knew
what colour their flowers are. I suspect most of them are white,
but as I also grow pink, red, sulphur and intermediate shades
they can be any colour. The one that is not so prolific is the
ordinary mauve wood violet. All are forms of *Viola odorata*.
The dog violets are distinguishable by their leaves and most of
them are pulled out, but in one part of the ditch there is a pretty
pink dog violet and I should hate to lose that. The purple-
leaved *V. labradorica* is always welcome. The leaves make a nice
patch of colour, and a thick planting can be very effective. This
violet has taken upon itself to carpet the bed where I grow a few
roses together. I will not call it a rose garden because other plants
are there too. Most of my roses are planted in the ordinary beds
among other plants and this is really the way I like to grow them.

Violas are as prolific as violets and they flower all through the
summer, so one ought to be grateful for them. But they are
rather untidy in growth when they grow big, so I pull out the
older ones. A little yellow and purple viola called Little Jock
seeds itself everywhere, and there are many others in shades of
blue, violet and lavender. Mr Bowles's Black Viola is a great
seeder, which is lucky as so many people want it. It is not really
black, but very dark blue. The different forms of *V. cornuta* seed
themselves too, particularly the white. I do not get many stray

plants of the mauve form but the wedgwood blue one is more generous. A friend told me how attractive *V. cornuta* is growing wild in the Pyrenees. He saw it with Welsh poppies and *Geranium phaeum* and it made a lovely picture. In another place there was so much growing in the meadows that it showed up over a mile away.

I never mind how many plants of *Alchemilla mollis* I find in the garden. The young leaves are so perfect that I hate to see them grow up. But the large plants are useful, for the roots are strong enough to make a barrier between bed and path. I have seen them making a wonderful finish at the bottom of a hedge and one could collect all the stray seedlings of grape hyacinths and use them in the same way, or even plant them with the alchemilla.

Another plant which sows itself generously but is big and tough enough to make an edging is the green Rose Plantain (*Plantago major rosularis*). A well-grown plant can be 18 inches across, and the flowers last for most of the summer. The beet-root-leaved plantain (*P. m. rubrifolia*) also grows into a fine clump, but of course has typical plantain spikes—the same colour as the leaves—instead of leafy green roses. *Brunnera macro-phylla* (*Anchusa myosotidiflora*) also makes a heavy clump, with dark evergreen leaves, that would make an effective barrier anywhere. Even in September there are stray sprays of tiny blue flowers.

Anyone with a shady garden would be grateful for *Claytonia sibirica*. It likes to sow itself under trees and in dark corners and makes most effective ground cover. It does not seem to have any regular time for flowering, for I find its small pink or white flowers at all times. *Corydalis lutea* is always in flower, too, and if we had no other plants we might feel more kindly toward it, for really its delicate glaucous leaves and yellow flowers are very pleasant. It can be allowed to stay if it decides to grow in a wall—and stay there. I found a garden recently where the white-flowered *C. ochroleuca* sows itself as generously as the common variety, but it does not do that in my garden. I regularly lose the aristocratic forms of oxalis but the cottage-garden *O. floribunda*, with rose-coloured flowers, gives me as many seedlings as I want. Now and again there will be a white one but this does not often happen. I thought I had lost the little yellow *O. valdiviensis*, after many years, but it has not deserted me although there is not as much room for it in the beds as there used to be, so it has taken to seeding in the walls.

When I was given a plant of the gold-variegated *Barbarea vulgaris variegata*, I guarded it as a great treasure. Now it seeds itself generously and makes large clumps which effectively fill large spaces with bright foliage. Mr Bowles' golden grass, *Milium effusum aureum*, is not quite so buxom but the seedlings soon grow big enough to make a cheerful patch under trees.

All the euphorbias are inveterate seeders and often put themselves in perfect places for good effect. Their green heads make pleasant summer effects under trees. Fennels, too, seed themselves rather lavishly, and while I agree one can have too many of them, either green or black, the small plants are easily removed, and if the big ones are cut down before they have time to seed you get a cushion of bright green or chestnut glinting bronze.

No one need have bare soil if they grow lamiums. The most prolific, of course, is the common *L. maculatum* with magenta flowers, but the salmon *L. m. roseum* sows itself too, and *L. galeobdolon variegatum* is irrepressible. But sometimes it shows real talent. When it wove itself through the skeleton branches of *Cotoneaster horizontalis* it made a wonderful background for the dark stems and red berries, and I can forgive it for many things when it works its way into a scruffy shrub and festoons the bare branches.

Many, many years ago a friend gave me a seedling of an apricot-coloured cleome and ever since it comes up each year in its hundreds and completely fills bare spaces between plants. Everyone asks about it and I give away endless plants, which I hope help their gardens as they do mine. Another friend gave me *Chrysanthemum macrophyllum*. It has really very attractive cut leaves in a light greyish shade of green. The flowers are ivory and could be taken for those of a tansy, in fact its common name is the Tansy Chrysanthemum. They last well in water and the plant is tough and bold enough for wild places. My first plant of *Artemisia absinthium* came from seed collected on Portland, and now I have all the plants I want. One can have too many, and there is a temptation to leave the robust silvery plants that always seem to find the best place to show up well. Most of the more refined silver plants have little to offer in the winter, but Wormwood is a good winter plant and can stand up to the worst wind and rain.

Not everyone likes the musky smell of *Phuopsis stylosa*, but there are those who find it pleasant. There is nothing wrong with the look of the plant. The green of the foliage is bright and fresh, the tiny pink flowers keep coming for weeks on end, and it covers large tracts of bare soil with its chance seedlings.

Everyone knows that valerian is a terrible seeder but it has its uses, and some of the self-sown plants give the touch of colour that is needed in certain places. *Eryngium giganteum* is clever in its placing, too, and one enjoys it longer because its bristling flowers change slowly from blue to silver and from silver to ivory, and are lovely all the time. Mallows are heavy seeders, too, and not all of them can be kept in the garden. The ordinary *Malva moschata* has rather a poor habit and the flowers are not the best shade of pink, but the white form is lovely, and improves every corner where it puts itself. I like it with yellow verbascums and white Pacific delphiniums, and with silver plants or green flowers it becomes an aristocrat. The fastigiate form of *M. alcea* is always pink, as far as I know, but it is a good shade of pink and when the plants reach 4 or 5 feet and are covered with flowers they will account for plenty of space. All through August, September and sometimes October they bring ravishing colour to the garden.

CHAPTER NINE

Foliage Borders

A border that is easy to take care of and can look attractive all through the year can be made entirely with plants that have good foliage. If some have flowers, that is an extra dividend, but most of the subjects are chosen for their good leaves. Different colours, different textures and different shapes all play their part. This is an idea that is gaining ground, particularly in large gardens. I was shown one at the Royal Horticultural Society's Gardens at Wisley not long ago and I think this will be an inspiration to many gardeners. With the current intense interest in flower-arranging, we are learning to use our eyes and enjoy the beauty of many quite ordinary things we have hitherto taken for granted. Once such a border is planted it will require very little work and, if care is taken, can be really colourful.

One of the plants I noticed at Wisley was the variegated form of *Vinca major*, *V. m. variegata* (*V. m. elegantissima*), which has wonderful leaves shining with health and bright with great splashings of cream and pale green. In this border it was planted under a tree and yet in many gardens it is regarded as too ordinary for consideration.

The shrubs I should think about first are those that are evergreen, and a few good conifers make a fine backbone. It is best to choose small slow-growing varieties for such a border and pick them for their shape and colour. A shrub I recently put in a long mixed border has received much attention, and I do not wonder because *Osmanthus ilicifolius purpurascens* is a handsome plant with dark shining foliage like a refined holly. The new growth is particularly attractive. The sarcococcas are a little brighter green but make a pleasing background, and for gardens that are not too exposed *Choisya ternata* has leaves which are the brightest green of all.

The best of the blue foliage plants is, of course, rue, *Ruta graveolens* Jackman's Blue, and to keep it neat and a good shape it pays to cut it back drastically in the spring. I am very fond of the blue-grey *Hebe cupressoides*, and it came as a shock that all my big plants were killed in the cruel winter of 1962–63. Since then I have seen most beautiful specimens in this area that survived the cold so I think it is a matter of planting it where it gets some shelter.

Nothing is better for a foliage planting than a big plant here and there of *Euphorbia wulfenii* or one of its near relations. The only way to be sure your seedlings of *E. wulfenii* are the real thing is to plant the parent by itself and then you know that all the little plants that appear are legitimate. If a different type is allowed near the named variety the future generations can be anything. I do not think this matters so long as one knows. I have had some lovely surprises from these stray matings, and the safest way to name such plants is *E. wulfenii* hybrid which covers every variation; and all of them are worth having. The nurseries are no luckier than private gardeners. I have had for *E. wulfenii* the brown-eyed *E. sibthorpii* and the compact black-eyed *E. characias*. This last is the one for a place where space is limited. *E. wulfenii*—if one gets the real plant—can be rather lanky, with its 5-foot stems. The one I was shown by an expert had orange 'eyes' and that is the characteristic I now look for. These euphorbias, with their glaucous leaves, are lovely all through the year. Good plants of *E. wulfenii* are particularly attractive in winter when the heads bend over preparatory to flowering and are looking the same way—then they remind me of a flock of long-necked birds.

After the blue-greys we come to the real greys—the rather light little leaves of *Hebe pinguifolia pagei* and the woolly leaves of *Ballota pseudodictamnus*. The hebe has small spikes of white flowers and makes a carpet in time. It is also good planted at the edge of a raised bed so that it hangs down. The ballota needs to

1. *Kolkwitzia amabilis* Pink Cloud. A graceful shrub whose arching stems look lovely, whether clothed with leaves or not.

2. Good value from around mid-April to November, dictamnus is attractive throughout and needs no staking. *Dictamnus albus* (*D. fraxinella*) is an elegant white form.

3. Colchicums flower from late summer and come up
year after year.

4. *Valeriana phu* Aurea is a valuable winter foliage plant with leaves of yellow-green which become dazzlingly gold by March, then turn again to green as the season advances.

5. *Clematis* Huldine has delightfully shaped flowers,
pearly-white inside and mauve below, and it should be
grown so that both colours are visible.

6. A musk rambler, Bobby James, has semi-double creamy-white flowers and a very strong scent.

7. *Paeonia lactiflora* Gleam of Light. *P. lactiflora* is the forerunner of many of today's garden peonies.

8. *Lathyrus latifolius* White Pearl. The perennial peas can
be grown horizontally and make interesting ground cover.

be well trimmed after flowering otherwise it looks bedraggled in the rain. I am always pleased when I can cut off the long flower spikes, which soon get untidy, although the tiny flowers which nestle in the woolly calyces all the way up the stem are pretty in a quiet way, and flower arrangers love them. *Atriplex halimus* is only semi-evergreen, but it keeps its grey leaves for a very long time. Although it does best by the sea it will grow quite well inland. More grey plants are found in the willow family, for instance *Salix lanata* and *S. elaeagnos*, but again they lose their leaves.

Artemisia absinthium is a tough, woody plant, which seeds prolifically and does extremely well by the sea. It is more grey than silver, but if you allow the flower spikes to remain all through the winter you get a large rounded clump, sometimes a yard and a half across, because the stiff flower stems can be 3 to 4 feet long and the tight silver mound from which they grow is 18 inches in diameter. All artemisia flowers follow the same pattern, tiny balls like miniature mimosa. In the improved form of the species, *A*. Lambrook Silver, the flowers are as yellow as those of *A. arborescens*, but not in *A. absinthium*. They start the same colour as the leaves but are a dingy snuff colour by winter. I usually cut them off and enjoy the domes of silver, but between stones round the lawn or for an occasional accent in paving I leave them for their shape rather than the colour.

There is no difficulty in finding evergreen shrubs with golden leaves, and for a small border I would choose *Lonicera nitida* Baggesen's Gold with its pleasant informal habit and slow growth. *Elaeagnus pungens aurea* will get rather big in time, but with me *E. p. dicksonii*, with the leaf colouring reversed (gold edging green), grows much more slowly. All the plants with golden foliage seem to be brighter in cold weather, and this is very noticeable with *Salvia icterina*, the golden form of *Salvia officinalis*. Three little plants I would use lavishly in a foliage border are the golden form of *Chrysanthemum parthenium* (which sows itself generously in my garden and always gets transplanted at once to act as a foil for silver plants), the bright golden grass

Milium effusum aureum, known as Bowles' golden grass, and *Valeriana phu* Aurea, which is dazzlingly gold in March but imperceptibly becomes greener as the season advances until by mid-summer it is like everyone else. For this reason, if the idea is to bring sunshine to any particular part of the border, it is best planted next to a deciduous golden-foliaged tree such as the golden philadelphus, *P. coronarius aureus* or the golden snow-berry, *Symphoricarpos orbiculatus variegatus*.

Silver plants for all-the-year-beauty need to be chosen with care. Some of the artemisias, such as *A.* Lambrook Silver and *A. stelleriana* are reduced to a bony structure in the winter. The helichrysums do not look much either, except in the case of the wide-leaved curry plant, *H. siculum* (*H. serotinum*), which makes a pleasant rounded bush if well clipped, or the little bushy *H. splendidum*. The santolinas, too, need to have been cut back very drastically in spring and all the dead wood and old flower stems removed in autumn. The whitest and most feathery is *S. neapolitana* or *S. n. sulphurea*, with pale yellow flowers. *Stachys lanata* is a fair-weather plant and can look very bedraggled after rain. I find the new form that does not flower, *S. l.* Silver Carpet, is, on the whole, a better winter plant and though it does sometimes develop spots on its leaves in very wet weather it does not look so much like a drowned rat as the other. In this connection there is another rather common plant that succeeds where the aristocrats fail. *Lychnis coronaria* is a good old cot-tage plant which seeds itself rather too much at times, but I collect those neat silver rosettes—the deep crimson *L. c.* Abbots-wood Rose or the white-flowered form—and plant them where I want reliable silver winter foliage.

The verbascums supply this, too, but on a bigger scale, *V. olympicum* or *V. bombyciferum* making rosettes almost a yard across and *V. haenseleri* (more silver than white) usually about 18 inches across.

Evergreen variegated plants are, on the whole, rather neat for an informal planting and look better as specimens among low plantings or in stone. I like the various forms of variegated box but they are either rounded or upright, and play the same role as the conifers. An unclipped plant of either silver or variegated privet is informal and far more attractive in this setting.

I cannot think of any really good red-leaved shrub that keeps its leaves, although the purple form of *Salvia officinalis* is evergreen. In places where it is reliable in winter the purple form of *Phormium tenax* is wonderful but even in Somerset it died in the bad winter. Now I protect it with shrubs to the north, south and west, not too big but big enough for protection. This is not the way I like to grow it, but I am hoping it will get big enough after a few years to stand alone. I know an enormous plant of the green-leaved New Zealand flax in a garden near London, which goes through every winter and sends up magnificent flower spikes and I have never heard that the purple form is less hardy.

There are one or two deciduous shrubs that will make contrast in the summer. It rather depends on the size of the border whether one chooses the purple filbert, *Corylus maxima purpurea* or the crimson-leaved sumach, *Cotinus coggygria* (*Rhus cotinus*) *foliis purpureis*, for that necessary deep accent. *Berberis thunbergii atropurpurea* gives the depth we want and for a small garden there is a dwarf form and the dwarf *Prunus cistena* is good perched at the front of a raised bed.

In a small garden one has to be careful, too. about the size of the deciduous variegated shrubs. Some of the cornus family are delightful but they get big in time. I know one good border where *Cornus alba variegata* (*C. a. elegantissima*) is planted to show up a purple-leaved berberis. After a few years the cornus has got so big that it swamps the berberis and dominates the border, which is not at all what was intended. I do not find that the variegated form of *Philadelphus coronarius* grows at all fast, though it needs a little careful pruning to keep it a good shape. The variegated *Kerria japonica* grows sideways rather than upward and the more adventurous layerings should be cut off with a sharp spade. Also a watch has to be kept for stems that revert to green. This happens with the golden snowberry too, but so far the smaller, less showy form of *Symphoricarpos orbiculatus* with a narrow silver edge to the green leaves shows no sign of making layers. I wish it would and I also wish that the silver markings were more distinct. It is almost too delicate in its slight variegation. The variegated bramble shows up well planted in the front of the border. It can be pegged down and the tips of the long trails given sand and peat to induce them to root.

If it fits the scheme to include one or two other small deciduous trees I think they should be those that make good silhouettes in the winter. *Rhus potaninii* makes a charming little symmetrical tree, with well-marked bark. It does run slightly and a few layers appear round it but it is not nearly as bad in this respect as the Stag's-horn sumach (*Rhus typhina*). These layers colour as magnificently as the parent tree and it is as easy to get good homes for them as for well-marked kittens.

A willow that stands out well above lower plants is *Salix babylonica annularis*, commonly known as the Ram's-horn willow. Its leaves are narrow, like most willows, and they fold back from the main vein, and curl round the stem of the shrub like a ram's horn.

The twisted willow, *Salix matsudana tortuosa*, grows rather big after six to eight years, and though its winter silhouette is one of the most lovely for the winter scene it needs plenty of room. There is another plant with twisted stems that is comparatively slow-growing but which needs careful placing. This is the contorted hazel, *Corylus avellana contorta*, which is not at all graceful when covered with foliage; in fact it looks rather hump-backed then and needs to merge with other things when in full leaf. In the winter no intruding vegetation should obscure its outline, every twist and turn of its warm brown stems should be seen. It is even more exciting when hung with its pale catkins. This was the bush that fascinated some of my visitors on an open day so much that they sought me out to enquire the name of the bush that had snakes running in and out of it. At first I could not think what plant they meant, but of course when I looked at the hazel again I wondered why the likeness had not occurred to me. The smooth brown stems are just like small snakes as they twist and turn in and out of the foliage, and the bush really does look as if it was inhabited by a big family of lively snakes.

Another deciduous tree that is delightful when hung with catkins is an alder, *Alnus incana aurea*. It does not grow very fast and has young shoots and foliage of yellow. The catkins are distinctly tinged with red and most colourful.

The white berries on *Symphoricarpos* Constance Spry are very large. They grow in big clusters at the ends of graceful arching stems and are a lovely sight throughout the winter.

The weigela with purple leaves is good in the summer but unfortunately does not keep them through the winter. *Weigela florida foliis purpureis* is a compact slow-growing shrub which makes a good companion for *Euphorbia wulfenii* or *Alchemilla mollis*. It has pink flowers which somehow show up the beauty of the purple leaves.

When the main planting of the border is finished there are one or two plants that can be introduced to cover bare spaces. Between green or golden foliage plants the small creeping *Euonymus fortunei* (*radicans*) Silver Queen with variegated leaves is slow-growing and very neat. Not so slow growing nor so neat, the lovely blue *Acaena adscendens* likes to skip about between shrubs and produces some very attractive colour schemes when it drapes its blue leaves against purple or lime-green foliage. The smaller blue-grey acaena attributed to the late E. A. Bowles has very dark stems and is not quite so colourful. I like it with bronze, the red-gold of the little conifer *Thuya occidentalis* Rheingold or *Hebe armstrongii*. The gold-variegated form of *Saxifraga umbrosa* or the gold and green variegated cress, *Barbarea vulgaris variegata* are lovely with grey or silver plants.

CHAPTER TEN

A Silver Garden

One part of my garden that takes care of itself is the silver garden. I did not really set out to make this garden because I grow silver plants all through the garden and find them indispensable for lightening borders and making pleasing patches in the winter.

Most of my garden is heavy clay, inclined to be difficult in wet weather and as hard as concrete in a drought. I have one patch, however, on a slight slope facing south where the soil is poor and though I have grown many things there, including vegetables, and enriched the soil, nothing has done well. Trying to think of a way of making the most of this bit of ground I thought of the silvers. Small plants set out in my heavy soil do not do well unless I can perch them on raised beds in full sun and I thought the poor soil of the 'Southern Slopes' would suit them well.

This part of the garden is below what used to be a small orchard, which now has a few shrubs planted in the grass. It, too, has a silver corner which makes a pleasant beginning to my little silver patch. A group of silver birches were put in several years ago to screen us from the houses around, and daffodils are planted under them. There is a carpet of *Lamium galeobdolon variegatum* under the birches, a lovely silver carpet that looks its best in the winter when the silvered leaves glisten with startling brilliance. The daffodils come up through the lamium and all I ever do is to cut off the heads of the daffodils and pull out handfuls of the lamium when it covers the little stone path and tries to carpet the lawn too.

There is an old apple tree in the silver garden and this, with the birches, gives shade at the top, while the rest of the garden basks in the sun. We never put compost on the soil here but we always follow our usual practice of planting with sand and peat, so the soil will be lightened in time—I hope.

The design of the garden is on patchwork lines, with irregular spaces separated by little paths of stepping stones. I am lucky in being able to get pieces of Hamstone tiles for this purpose. In the old days many of the local houses had their roofs tiled with large thin pieces of stone, each with a hole for hanging it on the roof. Though slightly irregular in shape they are roughly the same size and the pieces I get are about a foot across, less than a quarter of the original tile.

There are several advantages from making paths in this way. It allows us to walk on the beds whatever the state of the soil. The bits of stone can be lifted if weeds appear, and can be moved to alter the sizes of the planting spaces.

Nothing in this garden needs attention once it has been planted and watered well, except the tall artemisias. We cannot leave them out because one needs an occasional planting of tall plants among the many low ones. Many gardeners keep pinching out *Artemisia ludoviciana* and *A.* Silver Queen to stop them flowering, but this is a job that must be done regularly. It is much easier to wait till the plants are about a foot high and then cut them down to about 6 inches. If this is done their flowering is delayed and they make dwarf sturdy plants instead of untidy lanky stems difficult to control.

None of the regular silver plants need staking. Even *Artemisia* Lambrook Silver, with its great plumes of feathery foliage, needs no control unless it is grown too close to a lawn and has to be held up out of harm's way. The dwarf forms either make billowing clumps, as in the case of *A. canescens* and *A. discolor*, or cover the ground with silver mats as *A. pedemontana* and *A. schmidtiana* do. Most of the spaces in this garden are filled with plantings of smallish plants, but occasionally there is a big specimen of *Senecio* White Diamond or *S. maritimus* (*S. cineraria*); even they do not need staking, nor does *Centaurea gymno-*

carpa. The shrubby senecios, *laxifolius* and *monroi*, make
mounds of silver foliage and contrast well with the flat plants,
Chrysanthemum haradjanii (C. densum amanum) and *C. poteri-
folium.* The helichrysums make bushy plants of about a foot
high. The wider-leaved *H. siculum* is neater than *H. angusti-
folium,* which can be rather straggling. The shrubby helichrysum
which we used to call *trilineatum* or *alveolatum* has now been
named *H. splendidum* and though it never gets very big it can
grow to 2 feet and is remarkably hardy. In another part of the
garden I grow the semi-herbaceous *Clematis integrifolia* through
it. The dark blue hanging flowers show up well against the silver
foliage and as the clematis has very brittle stems this is a good
way to grow it.

The various forms of *Lychnis coronaria* which seed themselves about the garden are collected and planted together. I
always know which colour they are from their proximity to the
parent plant. The one that is most prolific in its seeding is the
deep magenta-pink *L. c.* Abbotswood Rose, and one tinged with
bright pink comes next. The pure white does not seed so much
for me.

I grow three different varieties of anaphalis in the silver garden.
The low and compact form I grow is *A. triplinervis* which does
not appear to me to differ much from *A. nubigena,* certainly not
enough for me to want to grow them both. *A. margaritacea* is a
runner, and I keep it to one side of the garden, and the tall *A.
yedoensis* to the other. This anaphalis is particularly good in the
winter for, like all the family, it holds its everlasting ivory
flowers for months, and with wide leaves up sturdy 3-foot stems,
it makes a striking picture. The leaves are grey above and silver
below, and fascinating as they flutter in the wind.

Glaucous foliage makes the silvers look even brighter so I
have several fine clumps of one of the *wulfenii*-type euphorbias—
I will not go further than this—and a good patch of *Othonnopsis
cheirifolia,* the blue-grey fleshy plant which delights in a hot dry
position and produces its yellow daisies—also fleshy—very early
in the year.

The foliage of pinks is also blue-grey and I have many of the old ones growing among the silvers, all started from small cuttings. There is *Dianthus* Thomas with double old rose flowers, and *D.* Brympton Red which has bright crimson flowers on foot-long stems. The rather cabbagy flowers of *D.* Rose de Mai in pale pink have a cottage look about them, *D.* Sam Barlow is an old one with a maroon centre on a white ground, while *D.* Argus is smaller with a crimson centre. There are laced pinks and the single white Chas. Musgrave, with a green eye, and its double form John Grey. The mule pinks do introduce a note of green into the silver theme. The one that does best in this garden is *D. multiflorus* with bright cerise flowers.

A glaucous grass which gives height and makes a graceful accent is *Helictotrichon sempervirens*. I like to see an individual clump planted among low-growing subjects. In this way one gets all the beauty of beautiful foliage, a graceful outline and arching plumes of flower.

Variegated plants are grown in other parts of the garden, but three thymes have found their way into the garden because they like the same hot dry conditions as the silver plants. *Thymus citriodorus* Silver Queen has the delicious lemon scent of this type, and white and pale green leaves. The golden-variegated form also belongs to this species, but *T.* Silver Posie is the variegated form of *T. vulgaris*. It has the typical 'stuffing' smell instead of the delicate scent of lemons.

CHAPTER ELEVEN

Bedding the Natural Way

The formal type of bedding, with edgings or whole beds carefully filled with well-grown annuals or biennials is not in keeping with carefree gardening. The growing of these plants takes time and trouble. Spaces to take them have to be cleared at the right time, and plantings so regularly spaced and evenly grown would look wrong with a natural planting.

But there is no reason why use should not be made of annuals if they follow the general pattern of the garden. When the other plants are interlacing and weaving into each other the humble little fillers must behave in the same way. In the bedded-out garden all these plants are grown so beautifully that they match each other in every detail, but self-sown seedlings and plants sown in situ vary considerably and a planting made with them is not monotonous.

One year I had great success with echium. The one I tried was the dwarf hybrid mixture, which contains many soft shades of blue, lavender and rose, giving a misty effect. I choose the biggest gaps between taller plants and cover the soil with sand or peat and scatter the seed. The annuals are thinned when quite small and then they make bushy plants which join up with each other and the plants around. In places where a distinct colour is better than a mixture there is *Echium vulgare* Blue Bedder, which is a deep bright blue, or *E. wildpretii*, which has pale red flowers. Usually a few seedlings come up every year afterwards in the same place and if too far apart I concentrate them to make a show.

Candytuft (*Iberis*) is another easy plant that can be sown where we want something to fill in between other things. Again

I prefer the dwarf mixture, or in dark corners the lovely white form, *Iberis umbellata albida*.

A good plant to fill dull places on a bank or in a rock garden is the brilliant blue *Convolvulus tricolor* Royal Marine. The flowers are exceptionally large and show up well against the carpet-like growth of the plant.

For brightening dull corners when the soil is poor a dwarf South African plant, *Cotula barbata*, is useful and easy. This has light green foliage and is smothered in summer with small round heads of deep yellow.

One plant that I never have to sow is the ordinary white *Alyssum maritimum* (which should really be called *Lobularia maritima*). Wherever it has grown the year before we get enough plants the following year to fill in all the gaps. It is just the right feathery plant to put among large dark leaves, and its faint honey smell is always pleasant.

There is one annual I always buy ready grown and plant near the front of the bed to make a carpet between perennials. The ordinary little blue lobelia, *L. erinus compacta*, looks hard and prim dotted at regular intervals among other bedding plants, but grown as an irregular carpet it becomes entirely different. As the weeks go by the plants grow sideways until they merge, and they are usually still flowering away when the first frosts stop the party. The one I like best is the pale blue called Cambridge Blue but I usually have some of the more usual deep blue as well.

Some of our parks bedding is done with foliage plants and they can be very attractive, especially when the planting is informal as a background for bigger things and not arranged in a geometric pattern.

I always like silver and gold growing together and as I have more large silver plants in the garden than golden ones, the demand is more for golden-leaved foliage plants. One of the most cheerful I have is the golden form of *Chrysanthemum parthenium*, which has dazzlingly golden foliage. Once planted it comes up regularly each year thereafter and I collect the seedlings and mass them under *Helichrysum serotinum* (*H. siculum*) and *Artemisia* Lambrook Silver.

It is in the winter that golden leaves are most appreciated, and that is when *Valeriana phu* Aurea is at its best. This actually is a perennial plant which is easily grown from seed. Early in the winter the leaves are yellow-green, but they gain colour as the winter advances and by March they are dazzlingly gold and dominate the border in which they are planted. They start going green in late spring, and by the time they produce their white flowers the whole plant is green and does not stand out among the other plants surrounding it. In addition to the colour the shape of the leaves is interesting. They start in a very normal way, rounded at the ends, rather like an erigeron. When they grow bigger, they look almost feathered, with deeply cut leaves rather similar to a centaurea. The plants can often be divided, and a small clump stretched to cover a square yard of bare ground by dint of diligent division. I have never seen this plant in any other garden except the one from which my first little plant was given and had never heard of it elsewhere. And yet when I went to Nottingham to speak to a large Flower Group and showed a picture of my plant on the screen a member of the audience said she knew a cottage garden which was full of it. Later I showed a slide of the rare double delphinium, Alice Artindale, and this, too, I was told was common in Nottingham, so I came to the conclusion that Nottingham was a place to go when one wanted unusual plants.

Sometimes a dark background shows up plants with light foliage. *Lavandula stoechas* makes a soft symphony of grey and lavender and as an underplanting I use *Hieracium maculatum* (sometimes called *H. praecox*) with pointed leaves so splashed with dark brown-crimson that they look almost black. *Perovskia atriplicifolia* is good with the hieracium too. Like all hawkweeds the hieracium seeds far too freely, so whatever else is left undone the seed heads must be kept cut or the whole garden will, in time, have a sombre carpet.

Among large glaucous plants of the *Euphorbia wulfenii* or

Ruta graveolens type a little discreet bedding with dark crimson foliage can help the scene. The bugle we call *Ajuga reptans metallica, multicolor* or Rainbow has metallic glints on its crimson leaves, and Mr Bowles' beetroot-coloured plantain is effective bedded out like this, and safest if the flower spikes are kept cut.

I have 'bedded' *Veronica gentianoides*—when it was dark glossy green foliage, I wanted—together with *Bellis* Rob Roy in shady corners; and *B. perennis alba* with other plants with yellow flowers or leaves. The gold-encrusted rosettes of *Saxifraga umbrosa aurea* make good fillings at the corners of beds where one wants something low and solid. Even the double Sweet William, *Dianthus barbatus fl. pl.* has been pressed into service to make a rich crimson setting for hazy blue nepetas or *Amsonia tabernaemontana*.

CHAPTER TWELVE

Taming the Exotics

There are some plants that look as though they belong to a different country. Most of our garden plants have been collected in different parts of the world but a good many of them seem at home when planted in our gardens.

I never feel that yuccas quite fit into an ordinary mixed border, although they are often used in this way. They are such valuable garden plants for isolated positions and special gardens that I do not think they should be stifled by domesticity. Wherever we plant them they should stand alone, for much of their beauty is in their spiky form.

There are two gardens I pass regularly where yuccas have been planted in grass banks, and there they look right and can be planted on a big scale and will need the minimum of attention I grow *Y. filamentosa concava* at the top of a flight of stone steps leading to a higher level and all the attention it gets is a stout cane (not to support the flower spike but to indicate to visitors that it is a flower spike and not a hand-hold as they climb the steps!), and its finished spike cut off after flowering.

Yuccas are good plants for a paved garden where they stand out to perfection, or in what I shall call—for want of a better description—a spiky garden. I know one such garden within a much bigger walled garden in Scotland and it is very successful —also labour-saving because all the plants in it take up a fair amount of space and none requires much attention.

There are many yuccas from which to choose, but probably *Y. filamentosa* is the one most usually grown. It gets its name, of course, from the thread-like strands at the edges of the leaves. The colloquial name for a yucca is Adam's Needle and the late

E. A. Bowles' name for the plant was Adam's Needle and Thread. Both *Y. filamentosa* and *Y. flaccida*, which also has thread-like hairs on its leaves, are dwarf as yuccas go—in this country at any rate. They seldom top 5 feet, whereas *Y. gloriosa* and *Y. recurvifolia* can reach 8 feet when they flower. But they do not do that every year; in fact one usually has to wait two or three years between each dazzling display and make do with the foliage. This is not as bad as it sounds, for both are magnificent even without their flowers. The stiff pointed leaves of *Y. gloriosa* form a magnificent rosette which can make part of a design. In *Y. recurvifolia* the leaves are longer and limp enough to turn back, making a striking pattern.

There are two kniphofias that go well with yuccas, in fact are sometimes taken for them. *K. northiae* has the same kind of massive beauty as an elephant. It does not even sit up straight like other kniphofias, but settles its grey-green bulk on the soil and produces enormous rosettes at all angles. The leaves are often a yard long, curved at the edges and making all kinds of attractive shapes. The flowers never seem quite good enough for such a mass of curves and glamour. They are no bigger than those on many more usual kniphofias, and my plant at any rate does not produce enough to make a show. The colouring is good, for they open from coral red buds to spikes of greeny-yellow.

Kniphofia caulescens is not unlike *K. northiae*, but the grey-green leaves are shorter and come in tufts at the ends of the thick stems. These stems have been compared to elephants' trunks. They lie on the ground and send down roots. In September there are stout flower spikes, starting a soft coral and later becoming a pale greenish-yellow.

Some people grow *Morina longifolia* in ordinary borders, I know woodland gardens where it looks at home, but it is also a plant that can stand alone or in the company of spiky, spiny customers. The great green rosette is made up of thistle-like leaves, which are somewhat prickly, although more in appearance than actual fact. The flowers are not at all like thistles. They are hooded and tubular and are arranged in whorls on stout 2-foot stems. To begin with they are white, but soon turn soft pink. After fertilisation they become crimson. I can never bear to cut off these handsome spikes because even when the flowers are over they are a most interesting design, with pouches of seeds packed round the stems instead of flowers. It would be more sensible to cut them for a dried arrangement because the first hard frost reduces them to slimy mush.

Now *Fascicularia bicolor* really is prickly and a plant of character if ever there was one. The one I know best is in the West Porlock garden of Norman Hadden and there it grows out of a steep background. I have never noticed whether this is a bank or a wall, as it is covered with interesting plants, with the large rosettes of the fascicularia as the central attraction. The long narrow leaves are barbed and the plant always reminds me of a sea anemone, for the flower nestles deep down in the centre. This stemless bloom opens its bright china blue flowers in late autumn and then the lower half of the surrounding leaves turn bright red. This, I understand, is in the interests of posterity, for the strange plant, which comes from Chile, has to be fertilised by humming birds. When I was given a small plant I was so anxious to give it a sheltered place that I pushed it into a hole at the bottom of a north wall with another wall at right angles. I cannot say it actually revelled in this position but it survived and does its flowering and leaf-turning act in a mild way, but not with the zest of Mr Hadden's. I do not believe it much minds if it has sun or shade, although most plants from Chile feel more at home if planted in shade with a chance of finding the sun, but should be given poor stony soil.

The eryngiums that come from South America are far less domesticated than the ones we usually see, with interesting spiny foliage and tiny green or mushroom-coloured flowers. The first to flower is *Eryngium bromeliifolium* with small pale green flowers lightened by white stamens. *E. serra* has wide leaves, like those of an agave, and the flowers are like big green thimbles 1½ inches in length. There is one even more like an agave which is called *E. agavifolium*, and grows to 6 feet. The spiny leaves are wider than the others, and there are spiny bracts on the stems where the small flower stems break. The flowers are green and somewhat bigger than *E. bromeliifolium*, but the plant is not completely hardy. Nor is *E. pandanifolium*, which flowers in late summer and has branching stems about 10 feet high. Its foliage is long and narrow and can be anything up to 6 feet long. The tiny flowers are little bigger than peas in a purplish shade and they make striking silhouettes. But pride goes before a fall and an autumn gale can easily snap the brittle stems, even if they are well staked.

Even some of the European sea-hollies have an individuality that makes them suitable for a special garden. The deeply cut leaves of *Eryngium bourgatii* are splashed with grey-white markings and the flowers are a delicate blue-green, with a silver sheen. The leaves of *E. variifolium* are not cut but scalloped, and have prominent white veins. The flowers are small and spiky in whitish-green and held proudly on straight 18-inch stems. I used to have difficulty in distinguishing between *E. alpinum* and its hybrids and *E. oliverianum* (which comes from the eastern mediterranean) until a nurseryman friend told me to feel *E. alpinum*. The blue thistle heads look as spiny as the others and it comes as a surprise to find they are as soft as the lace they resemble.

Grasses can be used in the same way as the spiky, spiny subjects. They need a position where they can tower above more lowly plants or as isolated specimens in lawn or paving.

There are several that are evergreen; first, of course, our old friend pampas grass, *Cortaderia selloana*, which should be planted in spring and given a commanding position. The Victorians knew something when they planted these majestic plants where they had a wide scene or a dark background, but they went astray when they crammed them into little front gardens. I like to see those ivory plumes, waving from the tops of banks or against sombre churchyard yews. In the smaller garden *C. s. pumila* is not too big, for it is 5 feet tall only, against the 8-foot of

C. s. Sunningdale Silver. The plumes of *C. s. rendatleri* have a tinge of pink in their silver, and are looser and less regular than the others.

The glaucous *Helictotrichon sempervirens* is on a smaller scale, but it is big enough to make an effect where its silhouette is not blurred with other things. The flower stems are long and graceful and blend beautifully with the leaves. Mr Bowles' Golden Grass, *Milium effusum aureum*, is evergreen, too, and does best in shade. I grow it under a big apple tree and am always fascinated by the seedlings, which are the same shade of bright gold although hardly bigger than a pin point.

Some grasses are not pretty in the winter. Gardener's Garters (*Phalaris arundinacea picta*) is flimsy and is soon shabby, so is best trimmed off, but all the varieties of miscanthus keep their shape and all they need is a little control if grown in a very exposed position. *M. sinensis variegatus* has much white in its striped leaves, and they get whiter in the winter, *M. s. gracillimus* has lovely leaves which are narrow and grey-green, and in *M. s. zebrinus* they are banded crosswise with gold. The flowers of the last variety are always rather late and they hardly have time to open before the first early frost, but they are lovely in their bleached state all through the winter.

One of the most graceful of the smaller grasses is *Molinia coerulea variegata*, with narrow striped leaves about 15 inches high, and graceful arching flower stems. This needs a smaller scene and is perfect in paving or above carpeting plants.

CHAPTER THIRTEEN

Your Shrubs as Hosts

There have always been gardeners who have allowed their plants to ramble through each other at will, but they have been the collectors who try to give their rarities the conditions they would have in the wild. Now, more ordinary gardeners are adopting the practice because we have discovered that this is an easy way to getting the natural, informal look we strive for in our gardens. The effects are better too, because the plants are far happier growing with each other than in isolation, and a happy plant is a healthy one. Left to themselves a great number of the things we grow immediately find another plant and work their way into it.

One sees how this urge for companionship makes the wisteria leave its appointed supports to attach itself to any nearby tree or shrub, the dwarf *Aristolochia sempervirens* we have planted as ground cover rears its head and uses the nearest plant for support, and the clematis much prefers to get into a huddle instead of spreading over the mesh we have provided. My husband used to spend much time untwisting the clematis tendrils which had clasped another stem of the plant and transferring them to the cold wire of authority. But the clematis continued to prefer the living support to the unnatural one, and every day the stubborn trails had to be patiently unwound and returned to the wire.

So if we can arrange for climbers to grow through other plants instead of training them artificially we save a great deal of time and get much more natural effects. Many of the plants we regard as wall shrubs look very attractive grown less formally. In New England Virginia Creeper, *Parthenocissus quinquefolia*, reaches the tops of the tallest trees. It also flings itself down banks and over stony outcrops festooning any shrubs it happens to meet on the way. The name, of course, refers to the shape of the leaves, which usually have five leaflets and turn the most dazzling shades of orange and scarlet in autumn.

What we used to know as *Ampelopsis veitchii* and which now has to be called *Parthenocissus tricuspidata veitchii* has autumn colour almost more dazzling. Its leaves are glossy and they vary in size according to the age of the plant. Instead of letting it loose on the house where it will—if allowed—cover windows, work under gutters, and get busy among the tiles—it is much safer and infinitely more attractive against a background of foliage. I have seen it where it has worked its way over a hedge and it was most startling in its brilliance. It will push through trees and shrubs and is magnificent on the highest branches. It makes colour in autumn in the same way that *Tropaeolum speciosum* shows up magnificently in the summer and justifies its name of Flame Flower. I know one garden where *Cotoneaster horizontalis* is used to fill a wide bed at one side of the house and it is here that the tropaeolum is growing, working its way in and out of the huge herring-bone fans of the shrub.

Once you grow the annual tropaeolum, *T. peregrinum*, you have it for ever unless you are one of those exceptional gardeners who does everything at the right time. Even if there was always time I do not think I could bear to pull out the long trails of yellow flowers while they still have colour, and of course a few seeds always find their way into the soil below and the following year we get this cheerful commoner festooning all the trees and shrubs it can find, and using tall perennials as supports if they happen to be on the route.

The mutisias are not very easy, and most gardeners find they do best if planted in good soil under a shrub that is not too dense and are then allowed to work their way up through the branches until they get through to daylight, there to open their daisy flowers. The mutisia usually grown is *M. decurrens*, with orange or vermilion flowers, but it is by no means an easy plant and definitely choosy where it will grow. A rather open shrub, such as philadelphus seems to suit it best. The leaves of *M. ilicifolia* have a look of holly about them, and the flowers are either pale lilac or pink. *M. oligodon* is rather like *M. ilicifolia* but more compact with flowers of clear pink.

Akebia quinata is a much more accommodating climber. It does not seem to mind where it grows and finds its own companions. It started on a wall in my garden but it soon found a buddleia nearby and transferred its embraces to that. This particular buddleia is the variegated form of *B.* Royal Red and the dark five-lobed leaves of the akebia show up well against the cream leaves. I have seen akebia covering an old brick pig sty, making use of the *Jasminum officinale* that was there before and somehow catching hold of the end of the branch of a prunus nearby and continuing its ramble through that too. The flowers of the akebia never show up very well, being dark chocolate-red, but they are pretty if one has time to study them.

Some of the fruits on climbers are almost more spectacular than the flowers. One of my ambitions is to keep a plant of *Cobaea scandens* through a winter. This plant is a perennial but not a hardy one and I think there should be places in my garden where there is sufficient shelter for it to weather a mild winter. I love the flowers of *C. scandens*, whether lilac or pale green, and one year was delighted to see the plant hung with large green seed pods. They lasted a long time—as long as the plant in fact—but not alas through the winter. I let cobaea loose on my wall, which already has more than enough cover with all the roses, clematis and ivies I grow on it, but the cobaea, like another good annual creeper, ipomoea, is happy hobnobbing with other plants.

The passion flower, *Passiflora caerulea*, is a perennial, but not a completely hardy one in all areas. I grow it in a warm corner but even in Somerset it does not always get through the winter, although it often breaks from the ground after it has been given up for dead. The corner where I grow it offers a variety of living supports, because it is a place where I plant small plants which

I want to keep under my eye, and when they grow up they remain in the same corner, which becomes rather overcrowded at times.

The worst offender at the moment is an undisciplined *Stauntonia hexaphylla*—an evergreen climber from Korea and Japan, where it climbs over trees. And that is where I think it should be. The small cutting I nursed so carefully has grown into an over-riding plant which is spreading in all directions. If it would make up its mind to climb up to the roof of the building it would be more popular than it is now because other climbers nearby—also grown from seed or cuttings—would have an easier time. The stauntonia likes to leave the wall and catch hold of every living thing in sight, and among its supports has found a large *Euphorbia lathyrus*, the tall stems of *Thalictrum dipterocarpum* and *Filipendula palmata* and brings with it the passion flower, *Vitis heterophylla* and *Clematis armandii*, all expecting to grow sedately through the stauntonia and add interest to the wall. Several friends of mine have lost patience with stauntonia and taken it out. They say the flowers, which are ivory with a violet tinge and scented, are not worth the struggle to keep this head-strong creature where they want it to grow. Fruits are not general in this country but occasionally there is a harvest. The fruit is an egg-shaped pulpy berry, about 2 inches long and flushed with purple.

Everlasting peas are good mixers. *Lathyrus latifolius* is a typical cottage garden plant, which is becoming popular again. It needs little attention and is useful for a labour-saving garden. In cottage gardens, it is the bright pink form we usually see, mingling with roses or jasmine near the cottage door. There is another with deeper-coloured flowers called Pink Beauty and a white, *L. l.* White Pearl. As well as growing up, these plants will grow down and make interesting ground cover wandering among low shrubs on the ground. *L. l.* White Pearl takes off a little of the yellow if planted among *Hypericum calycinum* and the two together solve the problem of underplanting a large conifer. The pink variety is lovely with dark foliage and shows up against *Mahonia aquifolium*.

Eccremocarpus scaber is rather a 'thin' plant by itself, but when it hides its long bare stems among the leaves of a shrub and emerges to hang down its trusses of orange, crimson or yellow flowers it is most effective. It seeds itself and now I have it growing through pyracanthus, ceanothus and *Viburnum fragrans* on my malt house. There is still a forsythia and a climbing rose, Pompon de Paris, waiting for it when it penetrates a little farther.

I was always rather worried about the lanky cottage chrysanthemums until I discovered by accident that they are quite happy growing through a shrub. They can grow extremely tall and even if one stakes early and well the stems are not very sturdy and it is difficult to get a nice looking clump. With my usual habit of planting rather too close together, a clump of the bronze cottage chrysanthemum found itself rather in the shadow of a *Helichrysum gunnii* which has grown bigger than I expected. This shrub has dark green foliage and looks like a heath until its little velvety flowers open, and then one realises what it is. The chrysanthemum pushed its way up through the shrub and flowered very well. The crimson flowers of the helichrysum had faded to soft brown by then, so the chrysanthemum was very effective with its dark green background. The pink chrysanthemum Emperor of China, or the old cottage yellow, can be grown in the same way, using any rather open bush as a host.

CHAPTER FOURTEEN

Clematis and Climbing Roses

More gardeners are now doing what nature has always done—using trees and shrubs as hosts for all manner of climbing subjects. Anyone who has seen *Clematis alpina* growing in Austrian woodlands knows how it rambles through any plant in its vicinity, climbing through briars and brambles, and falling gracefully over tree stumps and boulders. It looks enchanting growing like this; the flowers show up against the dark background and it is happy and at ease or 'relaxed', if we use modern idiom. Compare its graceful ease with the captive plants on our walls, tied to the wires we have arranged for their accommodation and losing half their charm by being coerced. As well as enjoying freedom of movement I think plants enjoy living with each other, and the clematis does far better when growing at close quarters with other plants.

The interest in clematis has grown enormously in the last few years and more and more people have changed the rather artificial way of growing clematis on walls for a more natural association. Clematis, we now realise, are extremely happy growing over or through other plants. We grow them up trees, through shrubs, let them wander among ericas or arrange them carefully on the top of low walls.

To grow them well up a full-grown tree means they must set off with a good start. Tree roots offer great competition and there is always the danger that the stimulants we give to our clematis find their way to the roots of the tree and not to the clematis. A very deep hole, about 2 to 3 feet away from the tree, is the first essential. Some rotted manure goes at the bottom, to be covered with good soil before the hole is filled in with a mixture of sand, peat and good soil, and the clematis is planted in this. I plant clematis on apple trees and pear trees, willows and specimen trees. One of my happiest efforts is the small-flowered rosy-red Margot Koster festooning *Prunus subhirtella autumnalis*. The particular prunus I chose is more of a shrub than a tree, with two main trunks branching from near the ground, which is ideal for the clematis for it means that the flowers are at eye level.

I usually try to arrange that the tree and clematis flower at different times, but I slipped up when I put a good form of *C. montana* up a judas tree (*Cercis siliquastrum*), for the two flower together. But the effect was good, for the white flowers of the clematis hung down in long trails from the lower branches of the tree. It was a mistake to put *C. viticella*, with its small nodding, purple flowers, on a weeping alder. The little dark flowers do not show up among the dark leaves, and a variegated shrub would have been much better.

Clematis rehderiana is a strong grower and it prefers to find its own means of support. It does not really matter what shrub it chooses, a viburnum, forsythia or even another clematis. My plant started sedately up a *Viburnum fragrans*, but that was not big enough to accommodate all the growth it makes in a year and it has now made use of a *Clematis tangutica* on one side of the viburnum and *Rosa × complicata* on the other. The flowers are the colour of primroses and have the scent of cowslips. They come in neat little upright sprays among the grey-green hop-like leaves.

Clematis with small flowers do not want to be grown too high above the eye. I let *C. texensis* Countess of Onslow, with its small pink pitcher flowers, trail down the top of a broken wall. *C.* Huldine has delightfully shaped flowers, pearly-white inside and mauve below. They are translucent and should be grown so that both sides of the flowers are visible. Let her ramble on a ceanothus on a wall that is not too high, and one gets a good picture of the whole plant. The pale hanging flowers of *C. campaniflora* are very small and delicate, but there are many of them and a dark shrub about eye level is the best way of showing up their pale charm of white suffused with the palest blue.

Roses and clematis are often used together. It is sometimes difficult to know how to treat the semi-herbaceous but extremely vigorous *Clematis jouiniana* and *C. j. praecox* (an earlier variety), for the growth in one season can be so luxuriant that it covers everything in sight. Trying to keep it within bounds on a wall means much work but allowing it to encircle the trunk of an old tree keeps it amused for a season. I know one garden where this is done and the effect is most satisfactory. The host is an apple tree which is not in the best of health, and is, I think, dying, but it is well enough to display two beautiful plants. *Rosa* Bobbie James is a musk rambler, named after the late Hon. Robert James of St Nicholas, Richmond, which has semi-double creamy-white flowers and a very strong scent. This rose has the first call on the tree's hospitality, and its long trails have disposed themselves in and out of the tree. In the autumn, when the rose has finished flowering, the clematis makes a fine display round the lower half of the tree. A patch of pink *Cyclamen neapolitanum* between its voluminous green drapery and the lawn completes a lovely autumn picture. The cyclamen take care of themselves and make a carpet of lovely marbled leaves after the flowers are over.

Sometimes a rose and a clematis make the climb together. On one of my largest apple trees I have the rose Breeze Hill wending its way to the top. This is not one of the really rampant types, such as Bobbie James or *filipes* Kiftsgate, but contents itself with a dignified ascent and has large double champagne-coloured roses at reasonable distances. I have planted the blue *Clematis* Perle d'Azur as a companion, for the clematis flowers late and does not start until after the rose has long finished. I think this is one of the best blue clematis, as it makes a tremendous show when at its best and the suggestion of pink in its flowers gives a pleasant warm feeling. We do not all have woods, and even if we had it is unlikely they would be on different levels, with steep paths so that one can look down on the plants below.

I have a friend who has such a wood and I remember going there once in early spring and looking down on a beautiful clematis which had flung itself all over the top of a tree below. I rather think it was a form of *montana*, but I have never checked on this.

Another friend has given her *C. orientalis* (Ludlow and Sherriff form) the freedom of an old apple tree. I visited the garden early in September one year and saw the clematis at its brilliant best. It had completely covered a rather low-growing apple tree and looked like a giant umbrella, hung with little yellow and orange lanterns with a background of sea-green ferny foliage. The Orange Peel clematis varies somewhat and some forms have flowers of a better colour and thicker texture than others. I had an old friend who was given one of the first seedlings of this clematis and she almost wept when she discovered hers was not as good as other people's. As clematis are sold in pots it is safest to choose your plant when it is in flower, if possible, before embarking on this species. After the flowers are over the seed heads hold on till it is time to cut it down in February. Winter rain and wet may reduce those silken tufts to wispy scraps, but when the sun shines they fluff out again to give charm and lightness to the plant long after the leaves have gone.

Clematis always enjoy being planted against a north wall and some never trouble to climb up and find the sun. After trying over and over again to please the lovely *C. florida sieboldii* (*C. f. bicolor*) at last I got it going really well under a north wall. It was making use of everything that happened to be growing under the wall, *Euphorbia lathyrus* and linarias and another clematis, *C. campaniflora*, with its tiny hanging flowers in the palest blue. The *florida sieboldii* was really happy and had put out stems hung with unopened flower buds and I visited it daily to see how it was getting on. I had to go away for two days and my first call when I got back was to the clematis. Alas, most of it had been cut off and there was one flower only left. Buds and half-opened flowers were on the ground and I never discovered which of my unexpected visitors had perpetrated the slaughter. Had an ardent flower arranger fancied the graceful spray or an enthusiastic gardening visitor felt it should be disentangled from the euphorbias and linaria and broken the stem by mistake?

Clematis florida sieboldii

I have grown the winter-flowering *Clematis calycina* (*balearica*) under a north wall for many years. It makes a mass of dark evergreen foliage, rather fern-like in shape and is sometimes called the fern-leaf clematis. The small greeny-ivory flowers are not at all showy, in fact their main claim for inclusion in the garden is that they bloom in winter. Some forms are a nondescript shade and all are spotted inside with maroon. It makes terrific growth and seeds itself about the garden. One seedling appeared under another north wall where I had already planted *C. viticella alba luxurians* which has small white flowers, with petals tipped with green, and dark centres. Like many of the clematis it seems to do better roaming over other plants instead of using the wires or trellis provided.

The small-flowered varieties of clematis are ideal for growing through other plants and after my mistake of putting *C.* Etoile Violette on a dark-leaved tree where it did not show up I planted it near the exuberant climbing rose The New Dawn. I have always felt that the very pale pink flowers of this rose were rather washy but they make an excellent background for the nodding violet flowers of the clematis, with their cream anthers.

The evergreen *C. armandii* likes a sunny sheltered position but it does not like to be grown in an orthodox way. It has a strong objection to being trained and prefers to find its own means of support and is happy when allowed to ramble among other things. In my garden it is growing next to a stauntonia in a sheltered south-east corner and has done everything but climb up the wall behind it. It is growing into the stauntonia and over a large *Euphorbia lathyrus* and a very tall thalictrum, and some stems have discovered that the water butt in the corner makes a good strong base.

It always comes as a surprise to see the large white flowers of *C. armandii* in March, and they are always bigger than I expect. They are scented, too, and grow in generous clusters. I once saw this clematis draping the top of a natural rock garden made from a steep stone bank. It had arranged itself into giant loops above the rock plants and the dark evergreen foliage made a good background for the flowers below. *C. a.* Snowdrift has larger flowers than the type and *C. a.* Apple Blossom has flowers of a delicate pink colour.

At the end of my double row of clipped *Chamaecyparis lawsoniana fletcheri* I planted a weeping pear to make a finish, *Pyrus salicifolia pendula*. On one side is an informal bush of the silver-variegated privet and on the other the tricolor form of *Polygonum cuspidatum*. When I planted *Clematis viticella* Kermesina—another small-flowered variety with rich ruby flowers—it was intended that it should work its way through the privet. The first year or two it did, but it turned its face from my garden and looked into my neighbour's, sensibly preferring a western outlook. Now it has found that if it clambers into the pear it faces south, and that is the way I expect it will go on. The polygonum has done the same thing on the other side and I get a most colourful picture of ruby-red, cream, pink and pale green against the silver-grey of the pear, which delights me for a month or more and needs no attention till I cut down the bare stems of the polygonum in winter and the clematis in mid-February to disencumber the pear. In a friend's garden this clematis is growing with *Buddleia fallowiana* Lochinch, against a pink brick wall, and is a great success. Here the two are flowering at the same time, but as a rule I try to choose plants that flower at different times.

I thought I had made a mistake when I put a *Clematis* Lady Northcliffe on one trunk of an elderly Williams' pear and *Rosa longicuspis* on the other. Good gardeners do not approve of trees that are allowed to come up from the ground with two trunks, but I am grateful that no one bothered about it when the tree was young, just as I am if I can find a silver birch doing the same. *C.* Lady Northcliffe may grow better for other people, but with me she hardly gets off the ground and does her flowering in the bottom half of the tree. I like to see the white stamens in her shapely flowers of Wedgwood blue, which is just as well, for she would not stand a chance if she had to compete with the rampaging rose. The two trunks of the pear are a perfect playground for the strong growing rose, and as the pear is very high it gives ample scope for a robust climber. When the rose is in flower the white blooms make snowy showers right up into the heart of the pear and the scent is quite intoxicating. It has beautiful foliage, too, and is a wonderful sight in the autumn when the leaves turn gold and orange.

Another of my many mistakes was to put *Rosa longicuspis* on the same apple tree (an ancient Blenheim with a mammoth trunk) as *R.* May Queen. The first few years were without worry, the Queen produced her lovely pink flowers—pink with a dash of lilac—all flat and quartered in the old way, and smelling divinely of green apples, while *longicuspis* was finding its feet. Now, of course I can hardly see May Queen, although she does most of her flowering low down and is much bushier than some climbers, and something will have to be done. The same thing would have happened if I had chosen *R.* Wedding Day, for this is another exuberant creature which needs a big tree to itself. Luckily I gave it one so I can enjoy its cream flowers without reservation. They open from deep orange buds and each petal is pointed. This rose has a strong scent, rather suggestive of oranges.

Better behaved are two double white roses, Sander's White, which might be a double white Dorothy Perkins, but is not so pushing, and The Garland rose, which has large trusses of double white flowers.

On a small apple tree I have a rose called Seven Sisters, which is interesting because of the different tints in the flowers. They are all shades of lilac-pink and range from deep colour to some almost white, but like many ramblers it has no scent. The foliage is a light green. Using a tree as host is an easy way of dealing with a very strong grower. I did not know how to control *R. soulieana*, which I grow for its blue-grey leaves, but it has been a success on a crooked old apple tree. The short sprays of cream flowers grow upright from the sloping tree, and show up well. There is a hybrid *R. souleiana*, Paul's Scarlet, which has single crimson flowers.

A good way to use an old orchard that is not too big is to plant various climbing roses on the old trees, and add interest by growing shrub roses in beds between them. A carpet of bulbs in the spring, one scything when the bulbs die down and great excitement when the rose season starts means little trouble and much pleasure. If possible there should be a good central path, gravelled or treated with a permanent surface, to save endless mowing.

Among the roses suitable for growing up the larger trees are the soft pink New Dawn, and the very similar Dr Van Fleet. Albertine makes a magnificent show when in bloom so it can be given a tree that has wide branches. The darker roses do not show up so well in trees that make a good deal of foliage and I should save the very old desiccated specimens for the vigorous

moss rose William Lobb, which grows to 6 or 8 feet, and the
vigorous Hamburger Phoenix, which is perpetual-flowering and
has bright crimson flowers. The creamy Alberic Barbier is most
accommodating and will grow on a north wall, so will do well
even in a bad position. It flowers early and has glossy foliage
which is always attractive. The rose-pink Mary Wallace flowers
later.

A rose that lends itself extremely well to tree or shrub treatment is the lovely hybrid tea rose Cupid. I expect other people
who have grown it in the orthodox way have felt a pole or wall
does not do justice to the most beautiful large single flowers of
delicate flesh pink. I have never felt that its foliage made a good
enough background for such beauty and the enormous orange
hips that follow. If the flowers have a large shrub with good
leaves as a background they really come into their own, and
something like *Garrya elliptica* or *Chimonanthus praecox* would
be better than a fruit tree.

CHAPTER FIFTEEN

Peonies

There is no flower more useful in the carefree garden than the peony. It can, of course, be argued that in some cases the flowering period is very short, and no one can disagree about that, but the peony has a great deal to give us in addition to its flowers.

The excitement begins very early in the year when the brilliantly coloured buds start poking through, bright crimsons and rich maroons, cerise as bright as a lobster's claw, and lovely shades of green. The developing leaves keep up their promise. Some lose their early ruddiness for more sombre green, but many of the garden hybrids—which flower last of all—have crimson stems and leaves almost until flowering time, adding rich colour to the garden.

Several peonies have most beautiful seed pods and these give colour for several weeks after the flowers have finished. Such species as *Paeonia mlokosewitschii*, *P. cambessedesii* and *P. russii* in particular prolong the season, for when the seed pods split they reveal the most gorgeous lining in the brightest imaginable shade of cerise. Cerise may not be the right name for the colour because everyone has their own ideas of colour. Cerise to some of us has a touch of magenta, to me it is the bright strong pink known as 'cherry', without a suspicion of blue, that is found in fuchsias and oriental rugs. Embedded in this brilliance are the seeds, jet black if they are fertile and a few dummies, the same colour as the lining, to confuse the novice.

The final dividend is brilliant autumn leaf colouring in the case of some varieties, and again it is usually the species that colour best. The single primrose flowers of *P. mlokosewitschii* are among the shortest lived but the leaves of the plant colour better than any other.

Some people put peonies in a border by themselves, which always seems to me to be a pity because even when the flowers are over the foliage is there and they are a great standby to give substance and a good background for other flowers—and their permanence can be useful in a labour-saving border. In a large garden I know, a wide border between a brick wall and an expanse of grass has peonies as a feature and I am assured needs very little upkeep. The peonies are at the back against the wall and the heavy semi-circular iron supports are left in position throughout the year. In front of them a pale pink floribunda rose flowers from July onwards, with cottage pinks making an attractive glaucous edging. The rose used in this garden is an old French variety now out of cultivation called Radium, which was propagated by cuttings. Nepeta could be substituted for the pinks but it would have to be well back from the grass.

The first peony that flowers in my garden is *P. tenuifolia*, with foliage so finely cut that it is sometimes taken for asparagus. If I were starting again I think I should be tempted to plant this peony in light shade, although I am quite satisfied by the way it increases in the sunny spot where it happened to land in the very early days of my garden-making. I was given a scrap of this peony about 1940 and put it for safety on the top level of a rock garden facing south. It has an old wall behind it and the drainage is unequalled and there it has sat ever since, getting a little bigger each year, occasionally losing an outside joint as I reluctantly chisel off fragments for the importunate. It does not exactly creep, but it spreads slowly and I am sure it will cover the whole of the top level of the rock garden by another 50 years if left in peace. My plant is single, in rich crimson—a little brighter than the old cottage garden peony. There is a double form in the same crimson and recently I have been told that there are pink forms too. I have not seen them yet and descriptions vary. I am not quite sure of the shade of pink. Gardening friends who have seen the treasures and hope one day to induce the owners to part with a fragment are lyrical over the colour. The owners, who are guarding their small plants from the covetous, are inclined to lack enthusiasm—'not a good pink' or 'rather a washy colour' are replies given when one asks about *P. tenuifolia rosea*.

It is usually some time in April when *P. mlokosewitschii* opens her creamy-yellow blossoms. They are lovely, if fleeting, and usually come out one at a time so the interest is sustained. The name bothers some people and this beauty is sometimes called 'mloko' or 'Molly the Witch'.

In my garden *P. wittmanniana* flowers after *mlokosewitschii*. At first I thought it was a late-flowering form of this plant but it is a rather bigger, coarser plant. The form called Perle Rose has cream flowers striped and splashed with crimson. When a big clump is fully out it is a fine sight. There are two other named varieties, Le Printêmps and Mai Fleuri, both with rich early foliage and soft pink shadings on the ivory flowers.

Some people seem to grow *P. cambessedesii* (which comes from the Balearic Isles) better than others. When I first planted it I had no complaints. The leaves are darker than most, with a crimson sheen which gives them a metallic look. It is usually rather a small plant with deep pink flowers and brilliantly coloured seed pods and looks well in an odd corner or some rather informal place. It is really not quite suited to an ordinary border. I grow it in 'the coliseum', a terraced bed we made when we scooped away earth that had filtered down against the house walls and was making that end of the house damp. The planting space here is narrow with walls behind and stones in front but it is an excellent place in which to grow special plants that must not be overlooked. It shares a bed with *Arisaema triphyllum*, double sweet rocket, one or two rather special double primroses, *Astrantia minor* and *Tovara virginica filiformis variegata*, all well behaved plants that will not take up too much space.

Not unlike *P. cambessedesii*, *P. russii* is a little bigger. It has the same dark leaves and cerise flowers and I find it does quite well in a lightly shaded pocket of the rock garden.

The leaves of *P. obovata* are magnificent in a deep bronze-red with a distinct bloom, and are particularly lovely in their early stages, although always distinct. The flowers can be rose coloured or white, and it is the white one I grow in a lightly shaded woodland setting. But, alas, those ravishing globes of pearly-white, with their golden centres, are very fleeting, and I always feel that the lovely foliage is given us to make up for the transience of the flowers. We wait a whole year to see them and unless one has very big plants with a succession of bloom the floral display is over in less than a week.

Paeonia obovata willmottiae is a named form picked out by that discerning gardener, Miss Willmott. It seems to be a little longer in the stalk, the leaves may be a shade darker in colour and the flowers perhaps a trifle bigger, but both plants are very lovely and I should be quite happy with the ordinary one only, had I not been given Miss Willmott.

Another peony to flower in May is *P. clusii*, which has finely cut foliage, large white flowers and golden stamens. The flowers are stained with crimson on the inside near the centre. It comes from Crete and is sometimes called *P. cretica*.

Paeonia emodii is another early peony, often flowering in March. It comes from Kashmir and has two flowers to a stem and rather pointed narrow leaves.

No one seems to be sure how *P. mascula* (*P. corallina*) came to grow on the island of Steep Holme. It is not thought to be a native plant. Though quite pleasant to grow among shrubs or perennials of a woodland type it is not as beautiful as some other peonies. It has rather deep pink flowers.

In *P. mollis* (*P. sessiliflora*) the flowers are deeper in colour and rather a magenta-pink, which shows up well against the blue-green leaves. It is not unlike *P. officinalis*, and is really more of botanical interest than garden merit. It flowers in May and so does *P. veitchii*, which is also interesting botanically and makes a pleasing clump, although the nodding flowers are not big. They are deep magenta-pink in colour, with pink filaments and cream anthers, and are well set off by the narrow-leaved foliage. *P. veitchii woodwardii* is an improved form; the flowers are bigger and more heavily stamened, and their colour is a good clear pink.

If the flowers of *P. veitchii* are small, those of *P. potaninii* are very small, at least those of the plants I have are. This peony has running roots and given enough space will turn up sometimes a yard or more from the parent plant. The foliage is very finely cut on straight stems about a foot high and it is a good plant to use as an under-shrub in woodland. I grow it in an ordinary bed and it has to compete with potentillas, a golden lonicera and striped iris, so it does not get far afield. I understand the type is deep red, but it is the white form that most of us grow. It has green instead of pink filaments.

Paeonia lactiflora is sometimes called *albiflora* and is the forerunner of many of the garden peonies we grow today. It is scented and has rich bronze foliage and stems. For those who like hybrids instead of species the one to buy is *P. l. whitleyi major*, a graceful and free-flowering plant with light single flowers in pearly-white, lavishly centred with golden stamens.

We used to call the single red peony that flowers in late spring *P. lobata*, but now it is known as *P. peregrina*. The great globes of blood red are most striking in a shady corner and they last in flower for some time. I grow it in sun as well, but I think the colour is more intense in shade. There are some named forms, Fire King and Sunshine are two, and there is also a form with pink flowers.

The old cottage peony, *P. officinalis*, makes rather a massive plant and is good in a border that is to take care of itself. It likes to be left in peace and the mass of dark green leaves is quite pleasant for most of the summer. When thinking of these peonies we probably picture the old double red first of all, *P. o. rubro-plena*. One sees it by cottage doors and the flowers last a very long time. My complaint is that sometimes there are not as many of them as there might be. I have a very good form of the double pink, *P. o. roseo-plena* but the old double white, *P. o. albo-plena*, has never done very well for me. Variations of the double forms can be quite exotic, *P. o. mutabilis plena* starts

Paeonia officinalis

rich pink and changes to white, and *P. o. rosea superba plena* has very large, very double light pink flowers.

Some of the single forms are lovely, *P. o.* China Rose is salmon-pink and has orange stamens, and *P. o.* Crimson Globe is the colour of a cabochon garnet, and has golden stamens. Perhaps the most exciting of all is *P. o. anemonaeflora rosea*, which has a petaloid centre. The stamens have become narrow strips and look like a bunch of ribbons, crimson edged with yellow, surrounded by rosy-red petals.

There are too many garden hybrids to mention, they can be single or double, often scented and in all shades from white to deep crimson. They are usually listed as 'Chinese Peonies', and most nurseries have good selections.

Tree peonies such as *P. lutea* and *delavayi* make quite big bushes fairly quickly and so need plenty of room. *P. lutea lud-*

lowii is particularly hearty in its growth and is best suited for a shrubbery or large empty corner where its beautiful foliage can be admired. The yellow flowers are small in proportion to its size and the nodding yellow cups do not stand out well. It grows easily from seed.

Paeonia delavayi does not grow as gracefully as *P. lutea* and is an ugly skeleton in the winter, but it makes a good-sized bush with rather darker leaves than *P. lutea*. At its best the flowers are bright glossy maroon, even sometimes almost crimson, but there are some poor forms with dirty brownish flowers which can be dingy.

The China tree peony, *P. suffruticosa*, sometimes known as the Moutan Peony, is the loveliest of all, rather slow-growing, with divided leaves that are almost fern-like. The large flowers are white with golden stamens and large maroon blotches near the centre of the flower. This peony is often crossed to give flowers of different colours, all large and beautiful—but rather fleeting.

CHAPTER SIXTEEN

Hydrangeas and Fuchsias

Of all the carefree plants we grow I would put hydrangeas and fuchsias high on the list. Both families can be guaranteed to give colour and interest from July until the first frosts of November.

To many people the typical hydrangea is the *hortensia* type. These varieties come in all shades from pale pink to deep crimson and are sometimes known as 'florist's types'. Starting to flower in early August they go on till November; in fact they are lovely until the first hard frost. There is an idea that hydrangeas do not like lime, but I am sure it is not so. Mine grow to enormous proportions in my pH 8 soil, in fact I spend the summer cutting pieces out so that I can see out of the windows. One is often advised to plant in peat. I think most shrubs do better if given peat when they are planted, and I always try to start my plants off well with a largesse of peat. Of course if it is blue flowers that are wanted peat can be added to the soil to make it more acid. There is a curious tendency to regard pink hydrangeas as rather common and there is a feeling that the best people grow only blue ones. My husband and I did not agree about this, but not from a snobbish angle, and there were no hydrangeas in the garden until he died and then they could be as pink as they liked.

I love the rich shades that one sees in some parts of the country where the soil is acid. In South Wales the banks of hydrangeas in all shades from pink to crimson and purple are superb, and to me much more satisfying than the thin blues produced by artificial means. A friend of mine who bought an old farm produced nearly as good an effect by collecting all the old iron lying about the farmyard and burying it under the bed where he planned to grow hydrangeas. Tubs filled with lime-free soil are a good idea if one wants variations in a limy garden, for again there will be variation in colour, and the deeper the original colour of the plant the richer will be the shades of purple and blue produced by the acid soil.

One is usually advised to plant hydrangeas in shade, and they do very well under a north wall. Care has to be taken to protect very young plants against frost, but once the stems have become woody nothing will hurt them unless too much soft growth is made by injudicious pruning.

As well as giving colour for months on end we are discovering how useful are the dried heads of hydrangeas indoors in the winter. Those with dark flowers are the ones most people want for this and some nurseries are recommending certain types such as Altona and Westfalen, which are very rich in colour by the autumn.

I grow hydrangeas under the north wall of my front garden and vary the theme with white-flowered forms and an occasional plant with variegated leaves. The best white is Madame Emile Mouillière.

Fuchsias are attractive among the hydrangeas in the front garden. The palest pink hydrangeas become pale green in late summer and then the hanging crimson and purple flowers of *Fuchsia magellanica gracilis* show up well and make pleasant contrast. The very pale pink *F. m. alba* would be charming with the darker coloured forms.

I have never made up my mind whether I prefer the lace-cap hydrangeas to the round-headed ones, and I think the answer is that the *mariesii* (lace-cap) varieties—Blue Wave, *lilacina* and the white *veitchii*—are good for a woodland planting, where they can sprawl as much as they like and grow as big as they like, but for an average garden with normal beds and plants that must fit in with other types I prefer the neater and more colourful forms of *H. serrata*, which are usually about 3 or 4 feet only and make neat upright bushes. In this section my favourite is *H. serrata* Grayswood, which has brilliantly coloured lace-cap flowers and crimson-flushed leaves. The small central flowers are often blue and the sterile flowers round the edge may start white but change to deep crimson or shades of pink or even blue. *H. s. acuminata* Blue Bird is a neat pink lace-cap which turns to blue at the least provocation. The ordinary round-headed types are good where there is plenty of room.

A recent introduction is called *H. s. acuminata preciosa*. It has round heads of brilliant pink and is unusually free flowering. I first saw it growing in the open dominating an irregular raised bed. It was covered with flowers and I was told had been flowering continuously for many weeks. It would be an excellent plant in a carefree garden, especially if it could be planted in association with nepeta or *Amsonia tabernaemontana*, which produces soft blue flowers over a long period.

Hydrangea paniculata grandiflora is an excellent plant for a mixed border. It flowers in July and has large panicles of creamy-white flowers, which turn to soft pink as they age. It can be cut back drastically in spring because it flowers on the new wood. *H. p. praecox* is not grown as often as it should be, for with its earlier flowering it lengthens the hydrangea season and its flat heads of sterile white florets are quite attractive.

The larger hydrangeas are particularly lovely growing in light shade. *H. villosa* does well against a north wall and will grow to 5 feet in a few years. The foliage is a silky greyish-green and goes perfectly with the large lace-cap flowers, which are a symphony of lavender-blue and soft pink. It is lovely when clothed in soft raiment, but rather gaunt and bony when all the glory has gone. The best specimen of it I have ever seen was in a north-west corner of a tall Victorian house. It was covered in bloom and I thought at the time its nakedness would not show up too badly in the winter. Another I shall never forget was in a woodland garden and it seemed to have made a bower for itself under overhanging trees. Here, too, it would melt into the background while waiting for the spring. I made a mistake when I planted one on the north wall in front of the house. It has no chance to hide its shame, and I cannot hide mine for having put it there. It is just by the gate and hits me every time I go in or out.

To me the Chinese *H. sargentiana* is less attractive; it is rather heavy with its dark velvety leaves and scaly stems. The flowers are enormous, in lavender and white, but they have not the charm of those of *H. villosa*. But *H. sargentiana* is a very handsome shrub which takes care of itself so long as it has shade and some protection in exposed areas. In a garden I know well it grows against a high wall with *H. villosa* and *H. aspera macrophylla*, another large-leaved Chinese species which grows to 8 feet. Its flowers are a happy blending of soft lilac-pink and porcelain blue. These hydrangeas have dwarf azaleas planted in front of them with heathers in the foreground, so it is a good example of carefree gardening.

The chief attraction of *H. quercifolia* is the magnificent way the large oak-shaped leaves colour in the autumn, but it also has white flowers, which are quite pleasant. It is growing in the same garden as the giants and on the same wall, but some distance away, hiding behind a yew hedge which encloses a small formal garden, and has for companions ferns and bergenias below and cherries above.

Hydrangea petiolaris climbs as well as any ivy. Put it on a wall or against a large tree and it will soon start its upward course. The flowers are white and quite attractive. It is one of those convenient plants that can be planted and forgotten and it does not balk at a north wall. I put it on the ugly stucco wall of a domestic addition and it has done its part well. When the leaves have gone the stems make a pleasant pattern which softens the starkness of the wall.

I always think of hardy fuchsias when I think of hydrangeas, because both flower in the later half of the year, both carry on without any effort until frosts put an end to their flowering, and hydrangeas and hardy fuchsias are one way of furnishing attractively a north border. These shrubs do not have to be moved so bulbs can be planted among them, and starting with daffodils one can go on to *Leucojum aestivum* and then to tulips, and by making a careful selection these will carry on till May and early June. Then one could have camassias, particularly the deep blue *C. esculenta*, and *Galtonia candicans*, which I think should be planted in groups among shrubs, and not dotted about among herbaceous plants in the open. I once saw it planted at intervals in a large rose bed and it was not a success. The pale green *G. princeps* seems to do better in the open in drifts on banks of light soil.

The fuchsias to plant with hydrangeas depend on the colour of the hydrangeas. With pale colours the rich tones of *F.* Mrs Popple show up well. Whenever I am asked to recommend a hardy fuchsia my first suggestion is always Mrs Popple. There is no question about the lady's hardiness, she goes through the worst winters without protection and her showy flowers of scarlet and deep violet are large for such a hardy plant. Some people cover their fuchsias with ashes or peat in the winter, even those that are recognised as hardy, but Mrs Popple needs no such treatment, although I never cut the stiff stems till spring.

Other hardy fuchsias include *F.. gracilis* (*F. magellanica gracilis*), which bears red and purple flowers on graceful stems, and its delightful variegated form. The leaves of this plant are silver flushed with pink and rose. The other forms of *magellanica* are hardy too. *F. m. alba* has the pink flowers which are rather small, although there are plenty of them. In *F.* Mrs W. P. Wood the flowers are bigger and it has to a certain extent superseded *F. m. alba*. *F. m. riccartonii* is the fuchsia often used as a hedge plant, and it is particularly attractive when the hedge is on a higher level so that the flowers hang down. The variegated form of this fuchsia, *F. m. versicolor*, is rather deeper in tone than the variegated form of *F. m. gracilis*. The leaves are grey-green and the variegation is of pink, crimson and cream, with an overall effect of deep pink.

There are two dwarfs which can be used in a rock garden. *F. pumila*, a miniature form of the species *magellanica*, is pyramidal in shape, with small red and lavender flowers. The flowers of *F.* Tom Thumb are large in comparison with the size of the plant, and perhaps a little brighter than those of *F. m. pumila.*

Though the growers refer to many other fuchsias as 'hardy' they usually recommend that the base of their stems should be covered with about 6 inches of weathered ash or leaves in the winter. I know gardeners even in Somerset who do this and then put boughs of evergreen shrubs on top. I never cover mine and I do not lose them, but they do not get away as quickly as those in my friends' gardens.

There is disagreement about the hardiness of Mme Cornelissen and I often hear news of her outstanding hardiness from most unexpected places, although I have lost her in bad winters.

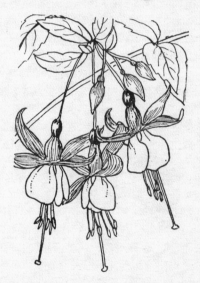

Fuchsia Mme Cornelissen

Her flowers of scarlet and white are quite outstanding, and *F.* Conspicua has the same coloured flowers on a shorter and bushier plant. Another good fuchsia with rose and white flowers is *F.* Alice Hoffman, also dwarf, and very free flowering.

In some gardens hardy fuchsias are used as bedding plants and *F.* Dunrobin Bedder is popular for this. The red and purple flowers are not particularly big, but they are numerous. As one would expect with such a name, *F.* Enfante Prodigue is a strong grower, with semi-double flowers of cerise and rich purple. There should be no question about the hardiness of Eva Boerg because it passed the test for hardiness in the trial at the Royal Horticultural Society's Garden at Wisley. It is semi-double in an attractive combination of white, pale pink and deep purple.

There are many other good hardy fuchsias which carry on without attention all through the summer until November.

CHAPTER SEVENTEEN

Varying the Heather Theme

Heather gardens are among the most carefree of any form of garden, but I do think they want brightening up with other things. Perhaps 'brightening up' is not the right phrase to use, for the heathers come in many bright colours which range from white and palest pink to shades of rose-pink, lilac-pink and crimson, but there is a kind of sameness about a lot of heathers growing together and I think they need a contrast or some taller plants grown among them. I like a few heathers here and there, but I never have had any desire for a heather garden as such. Heather growing on a moor does not have the flat effect of the average heather garden; for one thing the ground is usually very uneven and often large boulders crop up here and there, and such plants as blueberries and dwarf willows prevent monotony.

If the garden or border which is to be planted with heathers is very flat its contours can be changed, and a good way to do it is by using tree trunks, provided they are not too large and have been split in two. In one garden I knew where this was done colour contrast was obtained by encrusting the bottom of the tree trunks with sempervivums. Rather large ones were used, including the red giant *S.* Commander Hay, and the lovely *S. glaucum.* The sempervivums looked particularly good with *Erica vagans* Mrs D. F. Maxwell and nearby the bronze-leaved *Montbretia* (which I now learn should really be called *Crocosmia*) Solfaterra was tall enough to make good contrast with its smooth colourful leaves and fine upstanding flowers.

In the Munich Botanic Garden silver plants and other pale subjects including foxgloves, planted among the heathers, add much to their beauty. *Verbascum bombyciferum* is a most outstanding silver plant and with its enormous silver leaves in winter and tall spike of silver and gold in the summer it certainly earns its keep. Other good silver-leaved verbascums are *V. olympicum* and *V. haenseleri*. The first is a giant, with branching stems and yellow flowers. *V. haenseleri* is a more slender plant, with silver leaves that are not as felted as the others, and pale yellow flowers. I always find it hard to cut down the verbascums even when the flowers are long over and the leaves shabby, for the gaunt stems take on strange outlines which stand out above the plants below. They show up well above the heathers.

Another plant I noticed at Munich was the glaucous grass, *Helictotrichon sempervirens*. It is definitely a plant that should stand alone and, being evergreen, gives all the year beauty. Foxgloves have a lot to offer, too, their foliage is good—great greygreen rosettes all through the winter—followed by tapering spires of hanging bells. I do not know whether those at Munich are forms of the biennial *Digitalis purpurea*; the white form of this species is particularly lovely. *D. ambigua* is a perennial and has pleasant sulphur yellow flowers, while the crushed strawberry flowers of *D. mertonensis* keep coming over a long period. This foxglove is a cross between *D. purpurea* and *D. ambigua* and is usually only about 2 feet high.

In a garden in Dorset, where heathers are a great feature, one long, wide bed planted with various forms of *Erica carnea* gives a beautiful effect all through the year. In the front *E.* Springwood makes a lovely carpet, for the flowers with their brown anthers are large in comparison with some heathers and it mingles pleasantly with *E.* Springwood Pink and other heathers in shades of pink and crimson. Such a planting would look rather flat without something to break the monotony and this is done with different types of broom. There are many types of broom that can be used, but variations of the wild yellow broom, *Cytisus scoparius*, are a good choice, although they need careful planting. They dislike chalk and most alkaline soils and do best in light soils, which are dry and sandy. Always plant with plenty of peat and see that the beds are well drained. When thriving the bright green shoots show up well in the winter. Hard and regular pruning is necessary, particularly when the bushes are young, to keep them neat and rounded. Left to themselves they soon grow lanky and are very vulnerable to wind.

Even growing taller heathers with the low-growing ones does not have the same effect as introducing different types of plants. The tree heaths, *Erica arborea*, *E. australis* and *E. lusitanica* when planted among low-growing varieties help the flatness but not the dullness of too many heathers growing together.

In a large heather garden nothing is more beautiful than a silver birch, the bush type with two main trunks springing from the ground if possible. Among forms of *Erica carnea* a form of *Weigela florida* looks well, for instance the slow-growing *W. f. foliis purpureis* among those with light foliage, or the variegated form with *E. carnea vivellii*, the late crimson heather, which has dark leaves.

Dwarf conifers look right among heathers, but instead of putting in isolated specimens, a little group of say, five small trees planted together, is much more effective. The choice is more or less decided by the size of the garden. In a small space *Juniperus communis compressa* will be large enough. These little Noah's Ark trees are usually about a foot or a foot and a quarter high. In a shady garden the golden *Chamaecyparis pisifera plumosa rogersii* would be good.

Trailing plants growing among the heathers can be very effective. The climbing monkshood, *Aconitum volubile*, does not need a wall and I have seen the small-flowered varieties of clematis skipping about among low-growing heathers. Generally speaking, those with pale flowers show up best, such as *Clematis viticella* Little Nell or *C. alba luxurians*, with white green-tipped flowers. On light foliage one could use the crimson or deep pink forms, such as *C.* Kermesina in crimson or the wine-coloured *C.* Bountiful or *C.* Margot Koster, with deep pink flowers. *C.* Huldine is pearly-white and as much of her beauty lies in the soft shading on the undersides of the petals she needs to be grown where this is seen.

Some people might be shocked by the introduction of such plebian plants as the silver-variegated vincas, either *major* or *minor*, rambling among their precious heathers, but they add needed interest. I discovered that the golden-leaved honeysuckle, *Lonicera japonica aureo-reticulata*, is more attractive flitting about on top of other plants than growing on a wall. One I grew against a wall decided it was more fun to ramble and it now adorns lavenders and hyssops growing below. The gold-netted leaves show up well in the shrubs and are lovely in winter when they take on a pink tinge.

CHAPTER EIGHTEEN

The Fern Revival

Ferns are definitely coming back to favour and present-day gardeners are realising that their interesting evergreen foliage furnishes the damp, shady parts of the garden without needing any attention at all. Their leaves are among the miracles of nature and they belong to such a big family that there is almost no end to the varieties one can grow. Enthusiasts are beginning to collect ferns as others do grasses, primroses or rhododendrons.

Probably one reason why they have been neglected is that many of us who grew up with ferns had no desire to use them in later life. To me they used to be the lowest resort of gardeners, and I remember when we first bought our house and I was considering what exciting plants I should put at the bottom of a north wall in a damp bed, the young man who suggested it would be a good place for ferns nearly had his head snapped off. The Victorians have many things to answer for and the way they abused ferns is one of them. Ordinary ferns were often planted in the dank heaps of clinkers known as 'rockeries' and one also connects them with the gloomy shrubberies of that era. Owners of big houses did have delightful orangeries and conservatories built on to their houses, and here the rarer ferns grew in the right atmosphere with other tender plants, but those who had nowhere else to grow the indoor types filled up their bay windows with elaborate stands full of ferns, taking up what little light was left by the dark and heavy velvet curtains. As children we had to carry the precious ferns into the garden whenever a warm gentle rain was falling and I for one hated them as much as the canary, which had to be given a bath and have its cage cleaned. I suppose the ferns were watered regularly as well, but we were not entrusted with that nor the careful sponging of the leaves of the aspidistra.

The present aim is to make gardening as easy as possible and the fern enthusiasts of today grow them mainly as outdoor plants, although they have never lost their place in the greenhouse. But not everyone has a greenhouse and many people prefer hardy plants. Again the flower arrangers have shown us the light in favouring anything that has good foliage and particularly any plant that gives attractive leaves for winter decoration.

I do not think the present generation of gardeners will ever go back to the 'ferneries' of Victorian gardens, any more than they will start making moss houses, grottoes or shell houses, but ferns can be used in interesting features that fit in with our present ideas. I knew one gardener who made a delightful planting of the more exotic and rare ferns at the edge of a small natural pond in a shady part of his garden. An old lady who never lost her early devotion to ferns put hers under a big tree growing on raised ground. She made a series of terraces with split tree trunks, filled all the spaces with good leafy soil and planted a wide selection of ferns. To bring lightness to the greenery many small variegated ivies clambered about among the ferns and over the bark of the tree trunks.

There are many small ferns that can be grown in old walls; the less usual ones are worthy of a place in the shady rock garden or restrained woodland, and many ferns that are normally deciduous are found to keep their leaves when they get this VIP treatment. In my ditch garden I have several interesting ferns growing naturally in the steep banks. One is the holly fern, *Cyrtomium falcatum*, with fronds 2 feet long and dark leaves reminiscent of holly, and the hardy maidenhair fern, *Adiantum pedatum*. I have grown this for years, tucked into a crevice between stones on the east bank of the ditch, but it never seems to get bigger although it romps in other people's gardens. This is the American species with wire-like black stems and delicate maidenhair foliage, tinted with bronze when young. *A. venustum*, which comes from the Himalayas, is a slightly smaller plant and more like our greenhouse maidenhair. I have seen it grown with

FERNS

Above, left: *Adiantum venustum;*   right: *Cyrtomium falcatum;*
Below, left: *Phyllitis scolopendrium;*   right: *Ceterach officinarum*

hardy cyclamen, but I like it better by itself among stones. Two spleenworts have leaves like the maidenhair: *Asplenium adiantum-nigrum*, the black maidenhair spleenwort, which grows well in a wall or between stones on a steep bank, and *A. trichomanes*, which has narrow green foliage and needs very sharp drainage. It does well in a rock crevice with plenty of mortar rubble.

I get plenty of hart's-tongue ferns in the bottom of the steep banks of the ditch. *Phyllitis scolopendrium* likes heavy clay soil and sows itself in damp shady places. The lime-hating oak fern, *Dryopteris linnaeana* (*Polypodium dryopteris*) is planted in the peat garden and various other little ferns given to me by friends are happy below the pollarded willows that hold up the ditch. At long last, after repeated sowings and many plantings in various positions in the garden, the parasite *Lathraea clandestina* has consented to grow for me and covers quite an area under a willow—a live one, not a dead or dying willow which the plant is said to prefer—and its purple flowers look better with the softening foliage of small ferns.

Shady borders planted with ferns take care of themselves and ferns can also be used with other labour-saving plants. The airiness of their leaves contrasts well with bergenias and, interplanted with day-lilies, the luxuriant fronds of the ferns mask the day-lily crowns, which are hardly visible in the dormant season. Fern leaves dry remarkably well and make most attractive silhouettes against light walls in arrangements of dried flowers. Very often the colour of the dried leaf is very pale green and very pretty.

The names of ferns are not easy, and some of the smallest ones seem to have the worst names, but many have common names, like the hart's-tongue fern already mentioned, which is now *Phyllitis scolopendrium* but used to be *Scolopendrium vulgare*. It is an ordinary plant to many, as it grows so freely in shady banks in Devonshire and Somerset lanes, but it is useful for difficult places where nothing else will grow. It likes clay and has such shallow roots that it seems to perch on top of the soil in the steepest places. The long evergreen leaves look like ruffled ribbon, and they are longer and more drooping in deep shade but become more erect in the open. Fern collectors are always on the look-out for interesting forms of this fern and quite a number are available. In *P. s. cristatum* the ends of the leaves are forked, known by collectors as having a 'branched crest'. *P. s. crispum, undulatum* and *nobile* all have the edges of the leaves heavily frilled or goffered, and in *P. s. laceratum* the fronds are deeply cut and sometimes develop crests. Hart's-tongue fern leaves can develop ridges and a roughened surface and in the variety *P. s. marginatum* the edges of the narrow fronds are frilled as well. In *P. s. marginatum inequale varians* the fronds are also irregularly branched, making an attractive variation, and in *P. s. marginatum inequale muricate* the fronds are very dark green with the surface roughened and ridged.

Most people know the Male fern, *Dryopteris filix-mas*, which is the commonest wild fern we have. It has 3-foot, much-divided leaves which are roughly the pointed oval of a large sole. A very rare version of this fern is *D. f. fluctuosa cristata*, much smaller than the type, with crisped and crested leaves in dark green, and a stiff, erect habit.

The Lady Fern, *Athyrium filix-femina*, is somewhat similar to the male fern but in a smaller, more refined way, lacier, with a more curving design. It needs a rather damper position than the male fern and has many versions. One firm of nurserymen who specialise in hardy ferns has more than 20 different variations of the lady fern, crested, cruciate and twisted. One of the most striking is *A. f.* Victoriae with narrow crested pinnae crossing to form a lattice pattern.

The parsley fern used to be called allosurus but now is *Cryptogramma crispa*. It needs lime-free soil with humus, grit and a topping of lime-free chippings in the spring. *Blechnum spicant*, the Hard Fern, also needs soil without lime and its leathery leaves—divided only once—look particularly well hanging over water. Another lime-hater is the broad-leaved Buckler Fern, *Dryopteris spinulosa dilatata*, with large and handsome dark green fronds. It will lose its fronds unless conditions are particularly good.

One of the best-known ferns is *Osmunda regalis*, the Royal Fern, which is happy in any semi-shady moist position, but can be grown in the open if its great fibrous rootstock is in water. It is considered a lime-hater but cannot be too particular as it grows quite happily in my limy soil. The leaves are particularly exciting in their early furled stages, for they are shaped like croziers and have copper tints. This fern is sometimes called the Flowering Fern because the spore-bearing region of the frond is carried above the plant and looks like a spike of brown flowers. The leaves make good material for drying but care has to be taken not to damage the brittle main stem, the backbone of the leaf, and sometimes clever arrangers are able to strengthen it with fine wire.

The ostrich fern, *Matteuccia struthiopteris* (*Struthiopteris germanica*), gets its common name from the elegant way in which the young fronds unfurl. They are very pale green and do remind one of an ostrich plume. It likes a very damp position.

Onoclea sensibilis is called the Sensitive Fern, and it also likes to grow at the waterside or right in the water. Its leaves are pale green, and as thin as paper and against them the black spore cases, which cluster on separate fruiting spikes, show up well. It has running roots and can be used for ground cover in damp shady places. Again it has leaves that dry well.

Shield ferns (polystichums) are all beautiful and there are many very interesting forms of this British native. All like light shade and a soil to which leafmould or peat is added. After that they take care of themselves but if one has time to give them an annual topdressing of leafmould they do particularly well. An interesting form is *Polystichum aculeatum proliferum*, which has long fronds growing practically horizontally and carrying tiny young ferns along the length of the stem.

In *Cystopteris bulbifera* the bulbils are found under the leaves and sow themselves in cool, damp and shady conditions. This is quite a small dainty fern.

Other small ferns, suitable for old walls, rock crevices and at the edge of shady steps, are found among British natives. Once established they soon naturalise themselves and have a gentling effect on the stone. I can usually find little plants of Rustyback, *Ceterach officinarum*, in my old walls, also Wall-rue, *Asplenium ruta-muraria*. Both are pretty little tufted ferns. The first gets its name from the rusty-looking scales which cover the spores on the back of the leaves. The common polypody, *Polypodium vulgare*, has longer leaves, sometimes about 12 inches long but usually shorter. It puts itself in walls and also often grows on trees and rocks.

CHAPTER NINETEEN

Grasses for Easy Gardening

The interest in grasses grows, partly, I think, because they are such easy, no-trouble plants, which add enormously to the interest of a garden, and partly because of our growing appreciation of line and colour as an enhancement of the beauty of flowers.

Grasses have always been used for flower arrangement, from the pre-arrangement days when there were usually a few quivering grass heads among wild flowers picked for the house. Even today, with great experience and knowledge of the way to make all flowers last in water, wild flowers are proverbially difficult and in the old days only the grasses remained presentable in those pathetic little bunches. But now grasses are used with garden flowers, foliage and dried subjects, and are cherished for their airy elegance and flowing grace.

Grasses seem to fit into our idea of a carefree garden. We do not want too many of them and they need to be very carefully placed. I like to see them planted where a special effect is wanted, at the top of a steep bank for emphasis, tall ones in a flat planting to give height, arching varieties in pairs as a formal feature between one garden and another, and delicate-looking types as specimen clumps in small intimate gardens.

Some grasses make good ground cover and there are varieties for most parts of the garden. Some are frankly invasive and can be used only in wide, wild places, but in the right setting they can be very beautiful.

There is sometimes a temptation to plant one's grasses together as a collection but I do not think this is the way to grow them unless the owner is a collector with a garden run on museum lines. They are all right like this in a botanic garden, but not in private gardens which are purely ornamental.

As I feel that grasses are in two distinct classes, those that do not run and those that do, I think the best way is to discuss them in two sections, although some of the well-behaved types may not be quite so well mannered in lighter soils than mine.

Arundo donax is one of the biggest of the big ones and can reach 8 feet quite easily, with a comparatively slender girth, somewhere in the region of 2 feet across. The blue-grey leaves grow on alternate sides of the main stem and are wide and long and have a drooping habit so this grass makes good contrast with plants that are stiff and erect. I suppose it does flower in some places although I have never seen a flower, but that does not worry me because I grow it for its foliage and to make sure of that I cut it to the ground each spring. I do not think it minds if it grows in sun or shade but it does need a good setting, either as a monster specimen in an otherwise flat scene or given an inspired position against a dark background.

The variegated form of *Arundo donax* is a lovely symphony of white and light green, smaller than the type, but it is not hardy. I have had it and enjoyed its cool refinement in the summer, but I have not found the right place to winter it. Having no greenhouse I thought it would enjoy a wide sunny window sill in a mildly-heated bathroom (where geraniums spend the winter), but it never looked happy and showed no inclination to continue the struggle when it was planted out in May.

Pampas grass, *Cortaderia selloana* (*C. argentea*), is real victoriana but I see signs that it is not as strongly despised as it used to be. The Victorians abused its loveliness by cramming the biggest specimens into the smallest little gardens until one was sick of the sight of it—and of the dusty and often mangy 'plumes' stuck by themselves in a small and ugly container. Pampas grass wants room for its soft green arching leaves and the right setting for those great silky heads of flower. In the house, too, the scene must not be cramped, and the setting gentle rather than flamboyant. It should be honoured by a really important floral arrangement, with neutral shades that do not compete. It looks lovely against the old oak panelling of my dining-room with honesty and dried acanthus, pale golden achillea and blue-grey eucalyptus. The old ivory seedheads of *Allium siculum* blend well and I sometimes add the brown fronds of bracken or of the royal fern, *Osmunda regalis*.

I have clumps of pampas grass in several places in the garden, but the one I enjoy most is at the top of a flight of steps leading to a semi-woodland garden. It starts flowering in late autumn and is a wonderful sight all through the winter. I use the smaller type for this position but *C. selloana pumila* is not really small, reaching 5 feet or more. The type can be 7 or 8 feet and often looks its best in country churchyards against dark yews. There is one churchyard near me which is high above the road and has magnificent clumps of pampas grass. For a very big garden the tall and elegant *C. s.* Sunningdale Silver has no equal as it shows up well in the distance. When I think of pampas grass I remember two lovely gardens where they are exceptionally good. In Abbotswood, Gloucestershire, the silver plumes stand out amongst foliage of all colours, and at Sheffield Park they are reflected in water and companioned by brilliant winter colour. I do not know any garden in England where *C. s. rendatleri* does as well as in the south of France. It is not quite hardy but worth a trial, for its large irregular plumes have a soft pinkish tinge.

There are several good members of the stipa family with *S. gigantea* as one of the largest. It looks like a big colourful oat with purple and yellow oat flowers in large heads on 4-foot stems. The flower heads terminate in purple awns and the low tufts of grassy leaves can be regarded as ground cover.

Much less imposing but far easier to place, the Pheasant's-tail grass, *Apera arundinacea*, is a form of stipa but totally different. It makes a thick clump of fine graceful leaves about 2 feet high which become a mass of glinting bronze in the autumn.

Probably the most commonly grown of the tall grasses are the various forms of miscanthus. Zebra grass, *M. sinensis zebrinus*, is a wonderful plant if there is enough room for it. Though its official height is 4 feet it grows far taller than that in my garden. I like to give it a key position above lower plants, and sited so that the afternoon sun shines through it, lighting up the golden horizontal bands which intersect the length of the leaves. I wish the silky brown flowers would come a little earlier than late

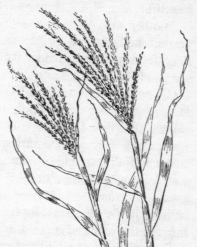

Miscanthus sinensis zebrinus

autumn because they do not always have time to open properly, but they remain through the winter and turn a warm ivory like the rest of the plant. I never cut my plants down till spring and find their tall and sturdy outline a pleasant winter feature.

Miscanthus sinensis gracillimus is a soft grey-green, with narrow leaves. It is well named, for it has great grace, more, I think, than the variegated version of *M. sinensis*. But this pale grass can make a happy picture with golden lonicera, *L. nitida* Baggesen's Gold, and the mahogany sedum, *S. maximum atropurpureum*. I do not cut these grasses down until the spring either.

The largest miscanthus is *M. sacchariflorus*, and this is so strong that it can be used as a screen in the same way as a bamboo. It does not run and its wide green leaves rustle in the breeze in a companionable way. I was given a golden form of this grass which seems to be less luxuriant.

Pennisetums are grown more for their bottle-brush flowers than for their foliage, which is not very exciting. *P. alopecuroides* has 3-foot stems and indigo-blue flowers in 5-inch spikes. The smaller *P. setaceum* flowers well, and its amethyst flower heads have a coppery tinge. They dry a greyish-brown but are still beautiful.

Another tall grass is *Spartina pectinata*, the Prairie Cord Grass. The best form for garden use is *aureo-marginata*, with its long ribbons of leaves striped with gold, and green flowers which are good for cutting.

Grasses in the 1½ to 2 feet class are probably the most useful in normal gardens and luckily there are plenty from which to choose. The one I should pick first of all is *Molinia caerulea variegata*, a very delicate variegated grass with slender arching stems. I think it should be planted where its shape can be appreciated from all angles and so should the beautiful glaucous grass, *Helictotrichon sempervirens*, which is about 1½ feet high without its flower stems. As its name implies it is beautiful all through the year and is useful for places in the garden which are bare in winter. I grow it between stones at the edge of the lawn and perched on a low wall at the back of a rock garden.

The panicums look well in a mixed border. This is the way they are grown by Mrs Norah Leigh (of variegated phlox fame), who gave them to me. One is *P. proliferum*, which makes a waving mass of slender stems and foliage in the autumn. In *P. virgatum* the foliage turns a rich reddish-brown, making a striking deep note among other plants. Golden timothy, *Phleum aureum*, is only a carpet of red-gold in winter but the summer growth is striking, with soft leaves striped lengthwise with gold. It is not a very tough plant and certainly not the kind which can be pulled to pieces and stuffed into odd corners with the expectation of nice fat clumps in a very short time.

The botanical name for sedge is *Carex*, and there are several that are useful in the garden and they do not insist on a damp position. *C. pendula* seeds itself all over my garden and has to be treated firmly. It is rather a coarse plant, useful in the rougher parts of the garden, where its evergreen leaves and hanging green flowers on stiff stems are always fresh-looking. *C. acuta* is even stiffer, with wider leaves and heavy upright flower heads. *C. morrowii variegata* has silver-edged leaves and is a much more refined plant. *Cyperus vegetus* does not need moisture as much as one would think, and I notice it seeds itself in ordinary flower beds, where it produces heads of bright green flowers throughout the season. *C. longus* is dark green with brown flower spikes and likes a moist position.

The woodrushes do well in dryer places and can make very good ground cover because they increase fast and soon make a dense mat. *Luzula maxima* (*L. sylvatica*) has bright green, rather wide leaves, and the form I grow, with silver-margined leaves, is quite an attractive plant. *L. nivea* has a more tufted habit, with soft grey-green leaves and fluffy off-white flowers on 2-foot stems.

There are not very many grasses with golden leaves and most of them are rather dwarf. Mr Bowles' golden grass, *Milium effusum aureum*, is an interesting golden form of our native wood millet, which is said to have been noticed by the late E. A. Bowles and was cultivated by him. It is evergreen and is at its best in spring when leaves, stems and flowers are all the same bright gamboge. It does well in shade and makes delightful sunny patches under big trees—the same sort of places where hardy cyclamen do well—and it seeds itself about with discretion. Mr Bowles also found a rush with golden stems. It is rather slow to increase in my garden and I have never had it named.

One of the neatest little grasses for the front of the border or even between stones in the rock garden, is the glaucous variety of Sheep's Fescue, sometimes called *Festuca glauca*, but more correctly known as *Festuca ovina glauca*. It is easy to propagate by division, does not spread or seed itself and looks nice all through the year. A good variegated dwarf that does not run is *Arrhenatherum elatius bulbosum variegatum*, with bulbous roots which form a tight mat below the white and green blades of the grass. A dwarf acorus which looks at home between stones on the lower part of a rock garden is *Acorus gramineus elegantis-*

sima, with rather a slanting way of growing, and narrow variegated leaves about 9 inches long.

These are the grasses we can trust and the others have to be
treated as potential dangers. *Holcus lanatus* is a pretty little
variegated grass which looks most innocent and sweet until you
put it in a special place and then you find it spreading and seeding over a radius of many yards. In a wild place it makes a very
pleasant patch of pale foliage. I like to keep the old variegated
grass, *Phalaris arundinacea picta* (Wedding or Ribbon grass, or
Gardener's Garters), cut to about an inch or two from the
ground when planted towards the front of a border though
it is allowed to keep its stems and leaves when used as a foil for
purple-leaved shrubs. It is a confirmed runner and wherever it
is planted it has to submit to the confines of a drain pipe or
bottomless oil drum. Even then it tries to escape by bubbling
over the top, but it is easy to cut it back to the line of the container. It is, of course, very attractive for cutting but its foliage
does not come on very stiff stems so it is rather untidy if left on
the plant to be buffeted by winter gales.

I have often wondered if the wandering ways of the striped
Glyceria aquatica variegata could be checked by planting it
in a fairly dry place. It was given to me as a plant for damp
places so I put it in the wettest place I have at the bottom of the
ditch, where water drains from the next orchard after heavy
rain. It is very happy there and roams far and wide, coming up
between stones and crowding over less rampant plants. It has
touches of pink in its white and green variegated leaves, about
2 to 3 feet tall, and is very pretty. I wish the variegated form of
the sweet flag, *Acorus calamus*, would grow as exuberantly. It is
not a grass, of course, though it grows rather like one, but a
rhizomatous plant, with bright pink colouring at the base of
the leaves and on the root. The leaves are narrow and stiffly upright and one gets the scent of tangerines by snapping a root in
half. This is not so barbarous as it sounds for each piece will
grow if pushed back into the mud.

The other really unmanageable grass is the beautiful blue-grey

Elymus glaucus, and it cannot be welcomed to any but the wildest company because it delves and runs without conscience. This is a pity, for it has great architectural beauty and a forest of it waving on derelict ground near water or as an anchoring plant in sand-dunes, can be quite useful as well as beautiful. When it flowers it is even lovelier, with blue-grey heads which, incidentally, dry exceptionally well.

CHAPTER TWENTY

The Garden in Winter

When I go round the country giving talks on gardens I stay in many homes and inevitably the talk turns to gardening. Many garden owners are worried that their gardens have so little to show in winter and those who are interested in flower arrangement would like more material for cutting. All find the sight of so much bare earth depressing and I am often asked for suggestions of what to plant. So I thought it might be useful to list a few plants that will combine happily with summer flowers and take away the bare, empty look of winter, without giving extra work.

The following lists are arranged in alphabetical order and I have made them short, without too much detail. This is easily obtained from nurserymen's catalogues.

CLIMBING PLANTS

Akebia quinata A twining plant with dark, five-lobed leaves and likes shade.

Clematis armandii This has white flowers, which are borne in April (there is also a pink variety) and dark evergreen leaves.

Hedera (Ivy) All these are evergreen. Variegated forms look well in dark places, and those with dark green foliage, such as *H. helix deltoidea* and *H. colchica dentata*, on light walls.

Lonicera japonica halliana An evergreen climber which has fragrant cream flowers in summer.

Rubus henryi bambusarum A climber with leaves rather like a bamboo, composed of three slender leaflets.

Stauntonia hexaphylla A vigorous Japanese twining plant with small pale violet flowers.

COLOURED FOLIAGE

Ajuga The glossy rosettes of Red Bugle, *A. reptans rubra*, or *A. r. multicolor*, show up well in winter.

Ferula (Fennel) This makes a mound of fresh fine foliage in very early spring in green or bronze.

Phlomis Soft grey-green leaves, varying towards white or soft yellow, make these shrubs valuable in winter.

Ruta graveolens The blue foliage is particularly good in Jackman's blue form.

Salvia Purple sage, golden sage and narrow-leaved sage all have foliage that is good in winter.

Tellima grandiflora A low-growing plant with round well-marked leaves, turning red and bronze in late autumn.

GOLDEN FOLIAGE

Arundinaria auricoma A dwarf golden bamboo, which is evergreen and best in an open position.

Cassinia fulvida Sometimes called Golden Heather, although more bronze than golden, this makes a neat, dense bush.

Chrysanthemum parthenium aureum A dwarf form of our native plant with very bright golden foliage.

Cupressus macrocarpa aurea This makes a useful change. There are several other good golden conifers.

Elaeagnus pungens aurea and E. p. dicksonii Both these have gold and green foliage.

Hebe This genus includes several with bronze and golden foliage; *H. armstrongii* and *H. hectori* are two.

Hedera Both small and large ivies include those with golden leaves, Jubilee and Buttercup are forms of *H. helix*, and *H. colchica variegata* has large leaves with golden variegation.

Ligustrum (Privet) The golden form is very effective grown by itself as a specimen bush.

Lonicera nitida Baggesen's Gold   An evergreen shrub that makes a good specimen bush.

EVERGREEN SHRUBS

Bupleurum fruticosum   With its blue-green leaves and yellow flowers this is good for exposed places and by the sea.

Camellia   These have wonderful glossy foliage and early flowers. They need lime-free soil and a semi-shady place.

Choisya ternata   Needs a sheltered border. Its glossy bright green foliage is aromatic and it has white flowers in May.

Conifers   These offer a wide selection of shapes, sizes and colours and a few in the garden help the winter effect.

Daphne laureola   A shrub which has very dark glossy leaves and produces green flowers early in the year. *D. tangutica* makes a neat rounded bush of small dark foliage with pink flowers in May.

Erica arborea   The tree heath, which will grow to 10 feet in time and needs a lime-free soil.

Fatshedera   A cross between fatsia and ivy, and has large glossy leaves and typical ivy flowers. Good tumbling down a bank.

Fatsia japonica   (*Aralia sieboldii*)   This has enormous flat leaves and cream flowers in late autumn, and will grow in the deepest shade.

Garrya elliptica   A shrub which will grow well on a north wall and has wavy grey-green evergreen leaves and long pale green catkins in winter.

Hebe Autumn Glory and Primley Gem   These make neat bushes and have good foliage and flowers in winter. *H. cupressoides* has lovely blue-green foliage.

Lonicera pileata   A low-growing evergreen shrub good for under-planting and ground cover.

Magnolia   *Magnolia grandiflora* has wonderful foliage all through the year and a specimen of *M. g.* Exmouth Variety, standing alone in a low-planted garden, is a wonderful sight in winter.

Mahonia These all have good evergreen glossy foliage; *M. japonica* flowers all through the winter and *M. aquifolium* in early spring. There are many hybrids.

Olearia ilicifolia A neat shrub with very dark, shiny leaves which stands out in a mixed border.

Rosmarinus The different forms of *R. officinalis* are hardy and evergreen, and combine well with stone.

Sarcococca Any of these dwarf evergreen shrubs are good, for they also have scented flowers in winter and take up very little room.

Siphonosmanthus delavayi With its dark green leaves, it sometimes gets its early fragrant white flowers damaged by frost and should not have an exposed position. Formerly known as *Osmanthus delavayi.*

Skimmia Shrubs which have bright red berries as well as handsome glossy leaves and do best in shade and lime-free soil.

Viburnum davidii It has very dark, large, evergreen leaves and *V. tinus* (Laurustinus) has white flowers in winter, as well as good leaves.

EVERGREEN HERBACEOUS PLANTS

Asphodeline lutea This has grassy foliage, in a greyish tone, and a big clump stands out well in the dormant season.

Bergenia Those species with large leaves, such as *B. cordifolia*, make excellent ground cover, often crimson-tinted, and such types as *B. delavayi* and *B. purpurascens* have upright leaves which turn completely crimson in winter.

Carex pendula Makes clumps of coarse grassy foliage which are quite effective when everything else is bare.

Cyclamen The marbled leaves of hardy cyclamen are good all through the winter.

Epimedium These may not all keep their leaves in perfect condition but *E. perralderianum*, *E. pinnatum colchicum* and *E. warleyense* do with me.

Euphorbia All the *E. wulfenii* types are beautiful in winter and flower in February, and among the smaller ones *E. myrsinites*, *E. amygdaloides* and *E. coralloides* are evergreen.

Ferns All these, particularly the easier types, such as Hart's-tongue and the Male and Lady Ferns, are excellent winter plants.

Fragaria These are evergreen with leaves varying from light green in *F. vesca* (*F. alpina*) to very dark green in *F. californica* and *F. indica*.

Geranium Most lose their leaves, but *G. punctatum*, *reflexum*, and *endressii* Rose Clair are evergreen.

Geum Some species and varieties have good evergreen leaves for winter.

Helleborus With the exception of *H. viridis* and a few rare species, these are evergreen.

Heuchera The foliage of these plants is attractive all through the year. *H. viridis* is dark green, sometimes turning dark crimson in winter.

Iberis sempervirens An evergreen with small dark leaves which are good for contrast.

Iris foetidissima The shiny leaves of this iris keep their shape well in winter. *I. japonica* also has good foliage.

Kniphofia caulescens This is a neat glaucous subject which stands out well.

Libertia An evergreen whose graceful narrow leaves look well on a bank.

Liriope Though small plants, they have grassy foliage, which is good in winter.

Phormium (New Zealand Flax) This is not hardy everywhere, particularly the more difficult types, but the broad pointed leaves of the ordinary *P. tenax* stand out well.

Primroses With their neat, crinkled leaves they are good for underplanting.

Salvia Many types, such as *sclarea turkestanica*, have magnificent foliage all through the year.

Scilla peruviana The Peruvian Squill has very bright shiny foliage through the year.

Symphytum These are evergreen and their matt-surfaced leaves are beautiful in winter.

Vinca The periwinkles, with their very dark, glossy leaves, make good winter ground cover.

FLOWERS

Apart from all the bulbous plants there are many flowering shrubs, *Chimonanthus praecox*, *Cornus mas*, *Garrya elliptica*, hamamelis, jasmine, *Lonicera fragrantissima* and *L. purpusii*, mahonias and *Prunus subhirtella autumnalis*, to mention a few.

Among the herbaceous flowers we have cyclamen, ericas, euphorbias, hellebores, hepaticas, *Petasites japonicus*, primroses and many pulmonarias.

STEMS AND SKELETONS

Cornus The ones with red stems include *C. alba variegata* (*C. a. elegantissima*) and *C. a. spaethii*, also *C. a.* Westonbirt. *C. stolonifera flaviramea* has ochre-yellow stems in winter.

Dipsacus fullonum This is the teasel and makes a wonderful winter skeleton.

Leycesteria formosa Worth growing if only for its smooth green bamboo-like stems, which show up best if grown slightly above the general level of the garden.

Perovskia atriplicifolia The stems are white in winter if the plant is not cut down till spring.

Onopordon acanthium This will keep its shape for many weeks until winds and rain ruin it.

Rubus cockburnianus (*R. giraldianus*) The powdered white stems of this plant show up well in winter. It has a running habit.

Salix The willows offer the best selection of coloured stems.

Sedum These, particularly the robust *S.* Autumn Joy, have strong seed heads in rich brown, and I never cut them off till spring.

PLANTS WITH VARIEGATED FOLIAGE

Arum italicum marmoratum The marbled leaves of this plant appear most conveniently in late autumn and last until spring.

Arundinaria I had given to me a small variegated bamboo, for which I have no name and which is good in winter.

Buxus There are several varieties of variegated box, in shrubs of different shapes.

Daphne odora marginata This has pale leaves, edged with silver.

Euonymus fortunei Silver Queen The creeping euonymus makes excellent ground cover in dark places, and several varieties of *E. japonica* have gold or silver variegation.

Fatshedera lizei variegata A good plant for a sheltered spot (see also p. 132).

Hedera (Ivy) All the variegated ivies, both large and small, stand out most magnificently in winter.

Ilex Variegated hollies show up in winter, the gold blotched Hedgehog Holly, *I. aquifolium ferox aurea*, is good in a small garden and others are larger.

Iris foetidissima variegata One of the best variegated plants for winter, as it is always sleek and unaffected by weather.

Lamium This is evergreen and *L. galeobdolon variegatum* in particular is startling in winter. *L. maculatum* is also good and flowers all the time.

Ligustrum (Privet) In either its gold or silver variegated form, it is very attractive in winter.

Phormium tenax variegatum and P. t. veitchianum Both have good striped leaves.

Vinca major variegata This has striking cream and green variegated leaves and is at its best in winter.

SILVER AND GLAUCOUS PLANTS

Cynara cardunculus The cardoon, and *C. scolymus*, the Globe Artichoke, make large clumps of silver foliage to go through the winter if cut down in autumn.

Hebe pinguifolia pagei This hebe has small glaucous leaves and never loses its well-fed look. It is a good plant to grow at the edge of a trough or wall, to tumble over the side.

Helichrysum siculum One of the 'curry plants', this makes a fine bush of silver foliage in winter. *H. splendidum* (*H. trilineatum*) is evergreen, with smaller leaves.

Lychnis coronaria This makes large rosettes of silver leaves in autumn for next year's flowering.

Pinks and Dianthus species These furnish welcome patches of blue-green foliage.

Santolina chamaecyparissus and S. neapolitana Both make silver mounds of feather foliage.

Senecio laxifolius and S. monroi Two silver-leaved shrubs which keep their leaves, and *S.* Ramparts and White Diamond are hardy silver plants.

Teucrium fruticans This has silver leaves but needs a warm position.

CHAPTER TWENTY-ONE

Strictly Practical

Even if we design our gardens with informality and plan to make them as easy as possible to keep attractive throughout the year there are still some jobs to be done, but these can be reduced.

For one thing I would not have any plants that need individual staking in a carefree garden—they are not in keeping anyhow. Some species can be used in a more dwarf form, the Belladonna delphiniums instead of the usual towering strains, the 3-foot *Aconitum* Bressingham Spire instead of the tall forms of *A. wilsonii*, and such digitalis as *D. ambigua* or *D. mertonensis* instead of the taller strains.

Some of the taller herbacous plants are easier to deal with if cut to the ground when about a foot high. If this is done their eventual height is much lower, and they flower later. Michaelmas daisies, heleniums and the taller solidagos can be treated in this way.

A garden planted informally where everything froths and billows together, would be really rather 'blowsy' without constricting hedges and some close-clipped conifers for contrast. The slow-growing hedges that need little trimming are the ones to choose, yew hedges grow slowly and never need clipping more than once a year. When newly planted they need light trimming to keep them dense. Box is the best for small hedges as it needs little clipping, and is particularly good in a chalk soil. It is seldom used for hedges over 3 feet high and grows very slowly. Unfortunately when we made our garden the hedges were made of *Lonicera nitida*, which is NOT slow-growing. When we were making the garden from scratch we were grateful for small-rooted cuttings of this obliging shrub, and as time went on made more and more hedge from cuttings taken from the original planting. They cost nothing and seemed a good idea. But they need constant attention and should therefore be kept small. This plant is quite unsuitable for tall hedges, and though the low hedges may have to be trimmed three or four times a year, the work is greatly decreased if they are kept compact. To do this means starting very early after planting to cut them back so that they thicken at the base. Always the base should be wider than the top, and to keep work to a minimum they should never be wider than a foot at the top.

The conifer I use to emphasise the walk up through my terraced garden is *Chamaecyparis lawsoniana fletcheri*, and though well over 20 years old the trees are still healthy and shapely. I keep them trimmed with an electric trimmer in April, and in August they are thinned. This consists of cutting out small pieces here and there to let light and air in to the main stem. This operation takes very little time, the holes are soon hidden with new growth and I am convinced the trees continue to prosper because of it. I spend much time convincing visitors that the work is done for the health of the trees and not for nesting birds.

In gardens where many shrubs are grown two tiresome jobs can be done in one. Instead of carrying away the leaves in autumn and using them for leafmould or compost they are simply swept on to the beds where they act as a mulch. A good depth is 6 inches all over. I would not like to do this with some of my rather small and delicate herbaceous plants, which could easily be ruined by slugs, but with shrubs, large primroses and ericaceous plants the system is a good idea. If in some gardens the birds insist on carrying the leaves back to the lawn the beds can be covered with wire netting.

Wide borders are more difficult to deal with than narrow ones but work is made much easier if there are stepping stones or a small path running midway the length of the border. This will not show when the border is planted and everything growing well, and it saves damaging the plants with tools and container and much trampling of the soil. If there is a hedge at the back of the border that has to be clipped a narrow path or a line of stepping stones is essential if one's plants are not to be ruined. One advantage of a narrow bed is that one can work on it from both sides without having to walk on the soil.

Most of my borders are next to stone paths and I always have the soil on the same level as the paths. The old-fashioned way was to raise the soil to a mound, and I am told that the reasons for this were drainage and to show off the plants better. Nowadays it looks quite artificial and out of date. When the border is next to grass, flat mowing stones help to keep plants back from falling on the grass and to give an uneven line in the front of the border. Here again the bed should be level with the mowing stones and there should be a gully about 3 inches wide and 3 inches deep between the grass and the mowing stones.

When it comes to cutting the grass one must avoid all small corners and banks which are difficult to cut. When I visited the Scottish National Trust gardens at Crathes Castle I was shown how prostrate conifers had been substituted for grass on steep banks at the side of steps. Bulbs in grass can hold up cutting operations for many weeks if the bulbs are scattered all over the expanse of grass. If the bulbs are concentrated in one place or around trees it does not add to the work. It merely means a wider sweep round the outside of the planting, leaving the rough grass in that one place until the foliage of the bulbs has died down.

In a very steep garden it saves much effort to have the piles of sand, peat and compost either in the middle of the slope or divided into two, with one supply at the top and the other at the bottom.

In a garden on different levels it is also a great help if paths are arranged so that the mower and barrow can be taken to any part without lifting them up steps. If steps cannot be avoided a ramp can be made at one side of them up which to push the mower and barrow.

Index

Pinks, 98, 137, *see also Dianthus*
Plantago major rosularis, 60
  m. rubrifolia, 60
Plantain, 60, 77
Polemonium caeruleum, 17–18, 57
  carneum, 18
  lanatum humile, 18
Polyanthus Lady Greer, 15
Polygonatum multiflorum, 15, 20
Polygonum companulatum, 18
  cuspidatum, 93–4
  vaccinifolium, 44
Polypodium dryopteris, 118
  vulgare, 121
Polystichum, 120
  aculteatum proliferum, 120
Poppy, 57
Potentilla arbuscula, 13–14
  fruticosa farreri, 13, 32
    mandschurica, 13
  Miss Wilmot, 16–17
  shrubby, 13–14
Prairie cord grass, 126
Primrose, 15, 99, 135, 139
Privet, 67, *see also Ligustrum*
Prunus cistena, 67
  subhirtella autumnalis, 89, 135
  tenella Fire Hill, 18
Pulmonaria, 16, 135
  angustifolia azurea, 16
  Munstead Blue, 16
Pyrus salicifolia pendula, 93

Red mountain orach, 58
Red: in foliage, 67
Rhododendron: azalea, 15
  praecox, 16
Rhus cotinus, see Cotinus coggygria
  potaninii, 68
Rock garden, 43–6
Rock rose, 43
Rosa Alberic Barbier, 96
  Albertine, 95
  Bobbie James, 90, **Pl 6**
  Breeze Hill, 90
  China, 50
  X *complicata*, 89

Cupid, 96
Dr Van Fleet, 95
filipes Kiftsgate, 90
Guinée, 48
Hamburger Phoenix, 96
Little White Pet, 33
longicuspis, 94
Mme Caroline Testout, 50
Mary Wallace, 96
May Queen, 94–5
Nevada, 31
New Dawn, 93, 95
on natural supports, 90, 93, 94–6
Paul's Scarlet, 95
Pompon de Paris, 87
Radium, 98
Sander's White, 95
Seven Sisters, 95
soulieana, 95
The Garland, 95
Wedding Day, 95
William Lobb, 96
Rose, 90–4, *see also Rosa*
Rose plantain, 60
Rosmarinus officinalis, 133
Royal fern, 120, 124
Rubus arcticus, 55
  cockburnianus (*R. giraldianus*), 136
  henryi bambusarum, 130
  variegated, 68
Rue, *see Ruta*
Rustyback, 121
Ruta graveolens, 31, 77, 131
  g. Jackman's Blue, 64, 131

Sage, *see Salvia*
Sagina pilifera, 39
  p. aurea, 39–40
Salix, 136
  babylonica annularis, 68
  elaeagnos, 65
  lanata, 65
  matsudana tortuosa, 68
Salvia, 131, 135
  icterina, 65
  officinalis, 65, 67